Soldier To Soldier

MAR   2010

Soldier To Soldier

Edd McNair

www.urbanbooks.net

Urban Books, LLC
1199 Straight Path
West Babylon, NY 11704

Soldier to Soldier copyright © 2009 Edd McNair

ISBN-13: 978-1-60162-173-3
ISBN-10: 1-60162-173-6

First Printing December 2009
Printed in the United States of America

10 9 8 7 6 5 4 3 2 1

This is a work of fiction. Any references or similarities to actual events, real people, living, or dead, or to real locales are intended to give the novel a sense of reality. Any similarity in other names, characters, places, and incidents is entirely coincidental.

Distributed by Kensington Publishing Corp.
Submit Wholesale Orders to:
Kensington Publishing Corp.
C/O Penguin Group (USA) Inc.
Attention: Order Processing
405 Murray Hill Parkway
East Rutherford, NJ 07073-2316
Phone: 1-800-526-0275
Fax: 1-800-227-9604

DEDICATION

This book is dedicated to my mom and dad, Evangelist Catherine McNair, and Retired Jumpmaster, Edward E. McNair of the 82nd Airborne Division, located at Fort Bragg, NC. May he rest in peace knowing that we love you, and that your three sons are still down here, carrying on your name with the same honor and respect that you did.

I am a soldier. I belong to an elite unit, and can be deployed anywhere in the world in 18 hours. If you drop me in foreign land, with my military training that I have perfected to a skill, and accompanied by my M16, no man can conquer me or my team.

I have been on many tours of battle, from Beirut to Desert Storm to Afghanistan, each of which made me stronger, and I've seen many soldiers fall. I've looked into the eyes of Iraqi soldiers and knew that they couldn't care less if I lived or died, knowing it would give them a pleasure to kill me, because they are willing to die for what they believe in, all in the name of Allah.

As I walk through these foreign streets, gunshots and bombs explode so close, I could feel the blast, and would choke off the soot in the air. I realize that my life could have been taken away at any time. Twenty-four hours a day, I wait for something to happen. I'd jump out my sleep, ready to attack, my nerves shot, unable to rest, for I am a soldier on foreign land, and I have one mission—TO MAKE IT BACK HOME TO MY FAMILY. Be-

cause I am somebody's son, somebody's brother, somebody's husband, somebody's father.

   I need understanding. I do this killing and conquer-
ing for the love of my country, family, and God. This is
my job. So as I rise every day and put on my camouflage uniform, tie my military-issued boots, throw on
my full battle gear, grab my M16 and head out, I pray
God allows me to survive another day.

Soldier To Soldier

Chapter One

On September 11, 2001, America was attacked. Our President and commander-in-chief said that he was sending his military to wage war on terrorism. At the time, I was stationed at Camp Elmore in Norfolk, VA. The Naval Air Station was right down Hampton Boulevard, which wasn't even a mile away. I was with an attached unit, a Marine Air Wing, where I and five other marines had to be for the next six months.

Norfolk Naval Base consisted of NOB and NAS. NOB is where all the ships dock, and NAS is where all the naval aircraft are stored, making it the largest naval base in the world. If a war broke out, this would be one of the first places our enemies would attack. So when 9/11 happened, I witnessed every base in the area go on HIGH ALERT—Fort Story, Fort Eustis, Little Creek, Oceana, and several more.

I was sitting on my bunk in the barracks when I heard the loud sound of the horn echo all over Little Creek Amphibious Base. I stood up with my eyes wide and flipped on the TV. The horn meant HIGH ALERT, and the base was locked down, so something major had happened. I turned the TV to the local news, and what I saw made my heart skip beats, and my chest get tight.

I stood and watched these planes crash into the World Trade Center. I listened as the broadcaster told the events, letting America know who the terrorists were and what they were capable of.

"This shit ain't supposed to happen," I yelled, balling my fist up.

Just then, my beeper went off, so I knew this was the real thing. I gathered all my gear and threw it in my duffel bag. I ran out the door and tossed my bag in the trunk. I walked outside and saw military personnel crying, others in a chaotic state, not believing what happened. But they were trained for different MOS (Military Occupation Specialist) jobs, not for war.

I kept my head and ran to Camp Elmore, where I kept all my gear. I rushed inside the big hangar, which had twelve bunks and housed twenty-four marines, and saw the other Marines I'd been sent to Camp Elmore with.

"Where the fuck you been? You better hurry up, or you gonna drive over there!" Sgt. Johnson said.

"Gotcha," I said, filling my other duffel bag and getting all my gear.

"This the real thing, Marines," Corporal Lyle yelled.

"Ooh-rah!" I yelled.

Every Marine in the hangar yelled, "Ooh-rah! Ooh-rah!"

That's when we saw Sgt. Harris, Sgt. Crawley, Corporal Reed come in the door, rush to their bunk, and began grabbing gear. Now all of us had come to Camp Elmore at the same time.

They called me, "Bigg." I was a lance corporal, and had joined the Marine Corps two years earlier.

Sgt. Johnson and Corporal Lyle were E-4 and E-5. They'd joined before me, but I knew these guys from high school. After moving to Virginia Beach from Fort Bragg my junior year, I had befriended them. I had always had my mind set on joining the Army and being a paratrooper with the 82nd Airborne, but hanging with my new friends changed my mind. They went in the Marines, saying it outdid the Army. I agreed, figuring I would outdo my childhood friends who all went into the Army. But they decided to be paratroopers and jump out of airplanes and had become part of the 82nd Airborne Division, stationed at Fort Bragg, an elite group of soldiers, and just being a Marine didn't beat them out or my dad. So I decided, before I went to Parris Island, that I was gonna be a grunt.

So I went to Parris Island to become a Marine. For three months, four drill instructors screamed, hit, beat, taught, shaped, and educated thirty young recruits into men, but only sixteen into Marines. Recruits quit, they tried to commit suicide, they cried, they refused to train, because Parris Island was a hellhole that broke you down then built you up into a well-disciplined Marine trained in hand-to-hand combat, an expert marksman and swimmer, with a sharp, well-conditioned mind and body.

After graduating from Parris Island, 2nd Battalion, Platoon 2001, I was a Marine. Then I went straight to Camp Lejeune, and was sent to Camp Geiger, where I would be in the field, going through extensive training for ground combat, and where I ran into Goofy and Junie. Goofy had become Sgt. Johnson, and Junie was Corporal Lyle.

It was in me to go all the way and be the best Marine I could and not just fall in the pack. So I decided to go with a Recon unit, which provided more extensive hand-to-hand training, straight killing, taking targets out, taking a hill, and more expert shooting with my M16. I felt I was ready for anything as a Marine, and so did Goofy and Junie. Side by side we went through hell.

Meanwhile, my childhood friends who were paratroopers were being sent different places. This was the end of 2000, and they were already in the war-torn Kosovo region of The Balkans. They told me they'd parachuted into Macedonia and moved in and secured things and brought peace. Now they were just rotating, making sure the peace was kept. The leadership threatened to send the Marines out, but a lot of Marines were still fucked up from Operation Desert Storm. So the only Marines getting sent out on missions were Force Recon Units, which comprised committed and well-trained Marines with every skill imaginable.

I was still training hard. I had taken karate earlier as a kid at Leigh Field House Gym on Fort Bragg. I had been training and earned my black belt in tae kwon do. I was chosen for a Force Recon Team, along with Goofy and Junie, who were determined not to let me outdo them. And I was determined not to let those paratroopers outdo me, so it was a straight shock to my childhood friends when I called letting them know I was leaving Fort Benning and had just finished jump school. Now they were sending me to Fort Bragg for six weeks of extra training.

I had to come train with 82nd Paratroopers, because they were the best, but when I got there, they had put me, Junie, and Goofy with a group of paratroopers called "The Golden Knights," soldiers who could jump out of a plane and land on a dime. So, by the time I left Fort Bragg, me, Goof, and Junie were hitting our spot, and we had our wings.

They took the set of wings with the two pins on the opposite side, placed it on my bare chest and hit it, making the Airborne wings stick in my bare chest and bleed. I didn't care. I was now a paratrooper, so I had it tattooed on my back, just like my childhood friends did.

In two days, me, Junie, and Goofy were standing in front of a gunnery sergeant on a shooting range out in El Toro, California. We would shoot from 0500 to 1700. This went on for five weeks, so I left there a sniper. I could take my M16, put my sling on my arm, sit Indian-style, rest my right elbow on my thigh, set my sights, and take the head off anybody at 400 yards, never missing. I received my sniper badge, while Junie and Goofy got expert badges and eventually had to go back.

But one of the major things I got from being in El Toro was, I was only there for a week. They sent us to Twentynine Palms, nicknamed "The Stumps," for desert training in 120-degree heat during the day and 45 degrees at night.

I was glad when we left to go to Little Creek Amphibious Base, Norfolk, where I would complete my Force Recon Training. Every day for two months, I would dive for hours. First we dived in a pool. Then we moved to the beaches. Next, we were diving in the Chesapeake Bay. Then they brought in Navy SEAL Team 5 to work and train with us for the rest of our time.

Then, as always, we were learning the strategies at

Little Creek in a class called "Strategic Analyzation." When we finished our classes, Sgt. Johnson and Corporal Lyle had to go back to El Toro, and they sent me to La Crosse, Wisconsin for cold-weather training.

As I lay in my tent on top of a flat mat, inside of a sleeping bag in 20-degree weather, I realized I didn't care about outdoing my friends. I had become one of the baddest motherfuckers in the world, and I could count how many there were like me.

I ended up at Camp Elmore in Norfolk after all my training, where I met Harris, Crawley, and Reed, who were finishing up their Force Recon Training with the diving. I was getting in more dives, which had become something I really cared for, so we all got tight, once Johnson and Lyle came back. We all trained together, stayed together, and most of the time, if you saw one, you saw us all.

Before anybody could leave out the hangar, Sgt. Major Goolsby walked in. "ATTENTION!" he yelled.

Everybody stopped what they were doing and snapped to attention, and you could hear a pin drop.

"Crawley, Sgt. Johnson, Reed, Harris, report to the Eisenhower. It's docked over at NOB. Lance Corp. and Corporal," he said, looking at me and Junie, "you two will be running with one of the SEAL Teams. Report to Little Creek."

"Sir, I thought I was supposed to go to Little Creek," Goofy said as we stared on, knowing that's what it was.

"Naw, this is the memo. You on the boat with them, and y'all two should have been gone." Sgt. Major Goolsby looked around the hangar. "This is for real, Marines. This is not a training exercise." Before leaving out, he added, "At ease."

"Y'all be safe and don't forget all we know!" I said to

my other three Marine buddies who had taken the extra step to become part of the elite.

"Ooh-rah, Marines!" Junie said to Crawley, Reed, and Harris. Then he and Johnson hugged. They had been friends since kids, growing up out Bayside Arms, and now they were going separate ways.

Junie left out, and I followed. We threw our bags in the back of his grey F-150 and headed to Little Creek.

We walked into the squadron to find several SEAL teams sitting and ready, waiting for orders as they came down. I sat there thinking about how the fuck this shit happened, not that I was worried, because this was what I was trained. I wondered if everybody was properly trained, since it looked like we would possibly have to go to war.

I pulled out my phone and dialed Sidney. He didn't answer, so I tried Bink.

"What up, Bigg?" Bink said, answering the phone.

"You know, ready to deploy," I said proudly.

"This is some serious shit."

"Yeah, fuckin' with people who don't give a fuck," I said.

"Naw, actually they do. They believe in certain shit, and they willing to die for it."

"Yeah, and they will kill 'em all. Let God sort 'em out," I said, all gung ho.

"You crazy, Bigg, but you sound like your brother Sidney," Bink said. "All he talking about is, it's time to get some."

"Where he at?"

"He don't carry no phone. He just check his voice-mail. He said he don't want to be contacted by mediocre people, that we were beneath him," Bink said, sounding offended.

I finally broke a smile. "Tell him to holla, soldier. When y'all getting out of there?"

"We confined to the base now, and all this shit just went down. Rob here with me. Sidney is unknown right now. And you know Fox was getting ready to get orders for Germany."

"Who he with now?" I asked.

"Fourth Brigade Combat Team, 508. He was with the 2nd Brigade. Remember 325th Airborne Infantry Regiment?"

"Yeah! I forgot he an officer anyway; his role is totally different. He told me he was with COSCOM now," I said in the form of a question.

"Know what, Bigg . . . you might be right, he was talking about Supply," he said, questioning his own words. "He ain't trying to get sent anywhere." Bink laughed.

"Let me holla at Rob," I said.

The phone went silent. Then, before answering the phone, I heard my old friend.

"I don't fuck with Marines. All they can do is clear the way when they see me open my chute," I heard as Rob came to the phone. "Who is this?" he asked, laughing.

"A real man, muthafucka. Talking shit," I said back. "You ready to go?"

"Am I ready? I'm eighty-second. I can be anywhere in the world, soldier, in eighteen hours, do a parachute assault, and secure shit. What?"

"Y'all soldiers do what you do. The country safe as long as eighty-second is around," I said, being smart.

"I knew you would come around. What's up, Bigg?"

"All good, partner. And you?"

"It's all good. Got a baby on the way, and they got me on alert. I ain't trying to go nowhere now."

"Congrats, soldier. Y'all believe in that family shit, not me, not now. I worry about y'all, man. I just want to make sure y'all go and come back safe," I said seriously.

"Got you, Bigg. You be safe, Marine, paratrooper, Navy SEAL, whatever the hell you are," he said seriously. "You and yo' boy be battling. Y'all go hard."

"Who? Sidney?"

"Who the fuck else? Nobody else doing all that extra shit. Rather be home with a shot of something in a glass, and a twelve-pack of something in the fridge. And a bitch ready to serve this trooper," he said without a sound, letting me know it wasn't a joke.

"Yo, man, I'm gone. See ya soon," I said in hopes that I would see Rob, Fox, Bink, and Sidney, all 82nd Airborne paratroopers and close friends I grew up with.

Fox became an officer. He'd gone to Fayetteville State and did his ROTC thing. Rob and Bink wore their burgundy berets proudly, but Sidney and I did look as if we competed a lot. But we were close, and it really wasn't that we were competing. Rob, Bink, and Fox never knew what truly made me go hard. They said I competed against Sidney, but he was older than me, and I tried my hardest to keep up with him.

I sat there thinking about how tight all of us had been since we were little boys living on Fort Bragg, the biggest Army base around. We went to Bowley Elementary together, Irwin Junior High, and Reid Ross High School. As my junior year began, my parents moved to Virginia Beach, but I made sure to stay in touch with my friends. My mom visited Sidney's mom quite often, and all her friends were still in North Carolina too. My mom and all her sisters in Christ used to sit around and pray for the safety of their husbands, who were 82nd. Now they were sending those same prayers up for their sons, who were getting ready to go into hostile situations, doing what soldiers do and what we signed up for.

Well, as it stood that day, nobody got sent out, and it would be months before I could be sent to Afghanistan.

March 2002, I landed on Bagram Airfield in eastern Afghanistan. I wasn't with a SEAL team; I was with a Force Recon Unit that was sent to carry out a pressurable entry, secure key points, and target military operations in the country.

What was supposed to be eight months turned into thirteen, before I had a chance to put my feet back on American soil. I came back and got into training, keeping myself on point. The things I'd seen, I didn't want to talk about. I became a PT nut and a real consumer of alcohol, trying to not think of Junie's death.

That day we walked in the form of a convoy, and as we moved slowly through Afghanistan in full body gear, a sniper sat within the walls. One of the first shots was to the Marine sitting on top of the 2.5-ton FMTV cargo truck with the .50-caliber machine gun. We went for cover, and the next shot ripped through Junie's left eye, and the bullet came out of the back of his head and hit the ground just before Junie fell back in that same spot. The entire team that went out with us, Harris, Crawley, and Reed were all ambushed by the Taliban and killed.

I was just glad to be back and was trying to get into the swing of things, but I had a slightly different state of mind and a fucked up feeling because, when I was leaving, I saw Sidney coming in. He was part of the 4th Brigade Combat Team, Special Troops Battalion. They were replacing the 101st Airborne Division, based in Fort Campbell, Kentucky.

We spoke briefly. I had nothing but encouraging words, until he told me he'd been to Iraq and none of this shit was gravy, so don't try and encourage him. For once, I didn't say a word. He was right. I was what you would call shell-shocked.

The rounds I'd shot off while in sniper school was nothing compared to several M16s firing, .50-caliber M2s going off, grenade launchers, and things being blown up around me, being the target of men, women, and kids I didn't know, and I had to make a decision to kill whatever and whoever ain't on my team. I may have started to panic and forget about my training. I choked. My friend was one foot away from me, and I had seen the round from an AK rip through his head.

I realized I would never make it out of there if I didn't utilize all that I'd been trained to do in a split second. I, along with a special team, pulled it together and made our way through hostile territory. It wasn't a success, because only ten of us made it, having lost two.

Chapter Two

I came home and took some leave. I wanted to get away from the base, so I went to my parents' home in Virginia Beach. My head was really fucked up. I had killed people to protect myself, but I knew I had also killed people who had no reason to die. I had taken the lives of innocent people, and I would see it over and over, not to mention seeing soldiers fighting by my side get wiped out in the blink of an eye, and having thoughts running through my mind that it could easily have been me.

The first week, my parents showed understanding, but my dad started growing tired of it, especially when he started drinking his Jack Daniel's and Budweiser. Though retired, this paratrooper still worked out every day at 0500, but this 5-10, 185-pound, 40-year-old paratrooper was no joke. I knew I had outdone him, so his accomplishments weren't so great any more.

As soon as I walked through the door, my dad said, "What up, son? Let me talk to you."

He and my mom were in the living room having a conversation. Budweiser in his hand, he sat down. "I need you to see me. Give up some change to help out around here," he said.

I knew this wasn't about money. He just wanted to show me I wasn't shit, like he always did when I was growing up.

"I give you money, Dad. That's no problem. What you need?" I dug in my pocket, pulled out about six hundred dollars, and waited to see his reaction.

Because my dad got his retirement check, another check for going to school from the military, and he worked another government job, his house, cars, and motorcycle were all paid for.

"I ain't gonna just take it, son. Let's do this," he said, taking off his shirt.

Growing up, my dad was that proud 82nd Airborne Paratrooper who excelled as Jumpmaster, 1st Sergeant, and had more jumps than anybody, but he was getting old. He'd always said that if you ever thought you could beat him in push-ups, then drop, and he'd give you ten dollars for every one you did. Nobody could ever beat him.

"You must don't want this ten. Because, you drunk, if you think you can still beat me, man. I ain't that boy who left here two years ago," I said, not wanting to embarrass him and hurt his ego. I loved and respected him.

"Stop talking. Before you drop down, I'll take two hundred on the light bill and be done. But if you drop, you know, ten dollars to the winner for every one. And that's because you not that boy who left here two years ago." He was standing in front of me and smiling, looking like he ate weights but never touched them.

"And don't forget, baby, because you must be drunk."
My mom rubbed her hand across Dad's six-pack and
smiled proudly.

I pulled off my shirt and asked if he was ready. We
dropped in the push-up position, head to head, and he
started talking. He talked for about three minutes, making sure I was ready. Didn't faze me, I was Force Recon.
This man had no idea what I'd been through.

"Ready."

"Stay ready. I'm a United States Marine. Ooh-rah!"

"I'm an 82nd Airborne Paratrooper, Jumpmaster!" he
yelled.

"Get him, First Sergeant," my mom said loudly.

"Count them, baby," he said. "Let's go!"

And we went down.

We were going at a steady pace, up and down, and
my mom yelled, "Twenty-five!"

My dad yelled, "I will always place the mission
first!"

As we kept going, his pace was steady, but I had
begun to catch my rhythm, and was feeling comfortable.

Then I heard my mom yell, "Seventy-five!"

My dad yelled, "I will never accept defeat!"

This was going good. I knew what he was capable of.
I'd seen him go all out. I knew he'd be dying soon, because I was starting to feel it in the shoulders.

But then his pace quickened, and we began burning
them out. He kept the same pace going as I stared in his
eyes. Then his eyes began to lose me. Our stares began
to miss each other, and I smiled.

My mom yelled, "One twenty-five!"

"I will never quit!"

That's when I realized he was still moving at an ac-

celerated pace, doing three push-ups to my one. I stopped and stood up, watched him burn out push-ups.

My mom yelled, "Two hundred, First Sergeant! Stop!"

He stood up and looked me in my face and said, "I
will never leave a fallen comrade, for I am and will always be a Paratrooper."

I stood looking at him, disgusted, not only with him,
but myself. How did I let this old man get me? And I
know he ain't gonna take my money.

I began to walk away. My mind had flipped. In fact,
my whole attitude had changed. I was mad at everybody, even my moms for playing his cheerleader.

"Hey! Can you see me?" my dad said.

"There you go," I said, pulling out my six hundred
dollars. I meant to place it on the table, but it fell out of
my hand to the table and floor.

I was getting ready to pick it up, when he said in a
calm voice, "Fuck is wrong with you? Pick it up!"

His stare was cold and unpleasant, which offended
me.

"I'm not a child, talk to me like a man."

"You acting like a child, throwing shit. Get your ass
beat like one. It's still like that in this house," he said,
stepping closer to me.

My mom saw what was coming and stepped between us and told me to go in the kitchen. Dad was
staring dumbfounded at me and my mom, as I walked
in the kitchen.

He stared at my mom like she was crazy. "You stand
right here, and if you come in there, it's gonna be me
and you. I mean it. Stay right here." He walked in the
kitchen right up to me and stared in my face. "What
she stop you from doing?"

"I'm not a kid no more, man. Back the fuck up off me!" I yelled.

His hand grasped my throat, so I grabbed his wrist and went to twist his arm and break it, but as I twisted, he shot around with an elbow that I thought broke my jaw.

The pain was so unbearable, I just lost it. I began throwing a flurry of fists on my dad, but he never fell, and he never stopped coming. I faked a punch, but threw a powerful kick that caught him in his side that would drop the ordinary man, but he caught my leg with his right hand and threw a left blow straight to my chest, which took all the wind out of me.

As I went down, he grabbed my neck and put me in a chokehold I couldn't break. I tried every tactic, but nothing worked, and my body began to crumble.

My mom yelled, "Stop, First Sergeant! You gonna kill 'im. Stop, First Sergeant."

I lay on the kitchen floor choking, trying to catch my breath. My mom was hugging me, wanting to know if I was all right.

"I'm good, Ma. I'm all right. Let me catch my breath." I tried to get to my feet, not knowing what had just happened. I yelled at my dad, "You flipping on me, man! You should be trying to help me. All this bullshit I'm going through, all the killings, and being over there, seeing people get blown up, birds coming down, soldiers dying while training, this shit is too much." I sat on the couch with my head in my hands. I was actually crying. I felt like I was going crazy.

My dad came and sat down beside me. "Look here, son. I know you think I don't feel ya, but I do. All those times I was flipping when y'all was young, it was because I was feeling the way you do right now."

I looked up at my dad as he talked.

"In eighty-three I was in Grenada, Operation Urgent Fury, 82nd, 2nd Battalion, 325th Airborne Infantry Regiment. I was there. Shit was so bad, they had to send in 1st Battalion, 505th Infantry and 508th Infantry. By the time my head was getting right from that shit, in eighty-eight they sent us into Honduras, Operation Golden Pheasant. We came in with the same mindset to fight, but we pushed the Sandinistas back into Nicaragua without killing nobody.

"In eighty-nine, I had to go to Panama . . . Operation Just Cause, a night-combat jump and seizure." He shook his head. "It was ran by a ruthless dictator, and we were trying to restore the newly elected government to power over there. And so that you know that I know about that desert, I did Desert Storm. I been to Iraq. I know about the heat during the day and the cold at night." He laughed.

"What about the snow?" I asked. "It snowed in Afghanistan?"

"No snow. Yo, man, you just got to take it one day at a time, one drink at a time. And if you need to talk to somebody, I'm sure the military got that for y'all young soldiers coming home," he said seriously.

"They ain't got nothing. Just deal with it, I guess. Just got to try and deal with it."

"Yeah, you right. Now get my money, I got business," he said.

I ran upstairs and got the other fourteen hundred, to go along with the six hundred, and placed it in his hand.

Chapter Three

Bink held his wife as he stood by the front door. "Baby, I'm just going to the field for a minute," he said.

"It's just becoming more and more often," Simone said sadly.

"You know, with all this shit going on, we got to be ready to go at any time. You married a paratrooper, baby."

Simone smiled, happy and proud of her little soldier. She grew up in Spring Lake, an area right outside of Fort Bragg, and had lived in Germany; Fort Benning, GA; and Fort Sill, OK. Her dad was in the Army, but he went 82nd, and was one of the "legs" (non-airborne qualified) at Fort Bragg. She had graduated from Pine Forest High School and met Bink after they'd moved from Oklahoma.

She'd dated a few guys in school, but when she came across Bink, who approached her in his camouflage uniform, his spit-shined jump boots, and his bur-

gundy beret slanted to the side, he had her overwhelmed.

Bink had just finished jump school, and was shop-
ping in the exchange for some new gear to wear out
later when he spotted Simone and her mom coming
out of the commissary. He watched her as he got into
his new 2002 Chevy Impala, rims glistening. He turned
up his sounds and watched Simone's mom run in the
exchange and leave her in the car.

Bink pulled over. "What up? What's your name?" he
asked.

"Simone," she said softly.

"How old are you?"

"Seventeen. Why? How old are you?"

"Nineteen. I don't wanna get in no trouble, 'cause
you all cute and whatnot, but I like you," Bink said.
"Can I call you?"

"No. I'll call you though. Give me your phone number."

Bink gave it to her, and she called it.

"Now you got mine. Lock it in, so you know when I
call. You better answer," Simone said.

"I will. When you calling?" Bink asked, going to his
car.

"Later on tonight, so we can go out," Simone said.
So I can ride around in that sweet-ass Chevy, she
thought. "You got a girlfriend?" she asked seriously.

"I do now," Bink said, smiling at her and her pretty
smile.

Simone called later and invited him over to her parents' home in Spring Lake, which was in the same
neighborhood as Sidney's moms.

Bink stopped by and sat and talked for hours. This
was just the start, because he visited her every day.

And her moms fell in love with him. It just so happened that she was a religious woman, into church, so when Bink invited her mom to one of our mother's prayer meetings, she enjoyed herself so much, she began visiting our mom's home church.

Bink, Fox, Sidney, Rob, and my mother, plus ten other ladies, would have prayer meetings during the day once a week at a different sister's house, but for some reason, Sunday was always at Sidney's moms house.

So Bink got close to Simone and took her to her prom in June 2002. He married her in September 2002 in a simple ceremony at Southern Pines Baptist. Fox was Bink's best man; they'd always had a strong connection. And Rob was just tight with everybody in different ways, always keeping the peace.

We weren't surprised when Bink told us he was gonna do it. Always laid back, he never wanted to go out a lot, preferring to just chill, lie low. Bink was a small guy with a lot of heart, tough as nails, always straightforward. Even though he only stood 5-5, 160, he had a powerful presence about him. Bink always said that, the day he saw Simone, he knew she was made for him, and that he was gonna marry her. And she would back him up by saying she saw him and made sure she sat her ass in that car that day. He admired her 5-1, 110-pound frame, and long, black hair that flowed with her dark brown complexion, her oversized lips, and pretty teeth.

Bink instantly used his VA eligibility to buy a home in Fayetteville over by Cross Creek Mall in a new development that was their Christmas present to each other.

They sat in their new home, sipping hot chocolate, enjoying the holiday love and cheer. They had spent a lot of time together since meeting. Bink wasn't trying to go nowhere without her, and she wasn't trying to let him. They were inseparable.

It was such a cold and heart-breaking day when Simone waited for her husband to walk through the door. She had some news for him that was gonna make him so happy and take him by total surprise.

Bink walked through the door about five o'clock. As he walked in, she told him to sit down. She took off his boots and put on his slippers, and brought him a Corona.

"I got some news for you, baby." Simone smiled.

"I got some news for you too, Simone," Bink said, being sarcastic.

"I'm pregnant—six weeks. I went to Womack Army Hospital today, but I'm gonna go to this private doctor my mom go to. But I am pregnant," she said, smiling her beautiful smile, rejoicing. "What's your news, baby?" she asked.

"I just got orders. I leave for Iraq next week."

Bink watched her smile disappear, and her eyes filled up with tears. She ran in their room and fell on the bed crying real hard, like a little girl.

Bink lay beside her and hugged her. He wanted to cry. At this point in his life, he wished he could quit the military.

On Wednesday, February 12, 2003, two days before Valentine's Day, 2nd Brigade Combat Team loaded onto the C-130 military transport aircraft and headed for

Iraq. Bink sat with all his gear, frustrated about the choice he'd made, but he was trying hard to settle in because this was his world for the next several months.

Bink looked over at Rob, who gave him a smile and a thumbs-up. He smiled for the first time. He knew Rob was ready. Rob was part of the 2nd Battalion, 325th Airborne Infantry Regiment, and they went hard. He was gung ho and seemed to be ready to do all he was trained for, and would definitely see action.

Bink was in the 2nd Battalion, 319th Airborne Field Artillery Regiment. He worked under Fox. He was a COSCOM soldier (Corps Support Command). COSCOM soldiers were responsible for arranging what the soldiers needed for war, from ammunition to all the equipment and supplies. Bink would be in Iraq, making sure that all the soldiers' weapons were ready and fully functional, all thanks to 1st Corps Support Command.

"So what's going on, soldier?" Rob asked, sliding in next to Bink.

"Ready to do my job and get back home," Bink said with a grim expression.

"We just getting going. Let's go see how they do it in another part of the world. These ain't the best conditions, but we gonna see some things outside of Fort Bragg. I know we going to war and we have the chance of not coming back, but we know that ain't gonna happen. So we take this shit as an experience. Bink, I just want you to see it different. We ain't going to prison." Rob laughed.

Bink smiled, letting Rob know he was gonna be okay.

"Man, we ain't been nowhere. We joined the military, and they send us right back home," Rob said. "Bigg from Hammond Hills, you and Fox from Anzio Acres, and I'm from Ardennes, all Fort Bragg kids. They call us military brats; now we got military brats of our own on the way," he said with a beam.

Bink grinned at the thought of his little man. "Picture that. We gonna be somebody daddy."

"Ain't that some shit. Ain't that some shit. Gonna have to ask Fox and Sidney for advice."

"Yeah! They been married the longest, and they got kids. They used to this family thing. I ain't scared to ask my boys some shit," Bink said, sounding a little better.

"We'll ask Bigg?" Rob said, and they both laughed.

They had a few more laughs before they fell asleep on the ten-hour flight into Frankfurt, Germany then to Kuwait.

Once in Kuwait, they had to wait to be shipped to Iraq, so they built a site up for tents, and that's how they lived for about a week before getting a C-130 cargo plane to carry them and all their equipment and supplies into Balad, Iraq.

They all had gathered with their company as the COSCOM soldiers unloaded the cargo planes and other equipment necessary for war. Once everything was organized, 2nd Brigade Combat Team convoyed into Baqubah.

As the soldiers fell into positions after gathering their weapons, Bink stood close, making sure soldiers knew their weapons, and how they functioned. Every soldier had an M16, and only the officers had 9 mm pistols, but Bink saw what Rob grabbed when he came through, and that was the M-249 Squad Automatic Weapon (SAW) with a belt (chain of bullets). The infantry soldiers that surrounded him grabbed the same, or M240B machine guns, M2.50-caliber machine guns, and massive amounts of grenade launchers, from the M203 40 mm to 60 mm, weapons that caused massive amounts of damage.

They moved in an organized military manner, watching everything that surrounded them as the HMMWVs (High Mobility Multipurpose Wheeled Vehicle), or Humvees, Jeeps, 5-ton cargo trucks, and military tanks moved at a steady pace into Baqubah. The heat beamed down on the soldiers wearing the light brown desert khakis, blouse and trousers, the tan desert camouflage boots, body armor, and vest to protect the groin and neck. With helmet, and light battle equipment, gas mask, and M16, these soldiers convoyed in full battle gear to the designated location, which they would make their home for the next six months.

For the first few months, when the threat level was red, the highest, it was full battle gear every day. When the threat level was Amber or Green, they could relax a little more, using just their weapons and camouflage hats.

Rob walked into his Contemporary Housing that housed four soldiers. These CHUs reminded you of a trailer, but it worked as long as he got a hot meal. He put up his gear and walked out to the DFAC (chow hall) for a bite to eat.

In the next six months, Rob's battalion organized combat operations everywhere in Iraq.

Rob prepared to go home along with Bink in August

2003, when 3rd Brigade Combat Team came in to take over, but separate battalions were sent home, which included Bink, but Rob and the rest of 2nd BCT stayed in Iraq, attached to 1st Armored Division, and kept on organizing Operation Iraqi Freedom.

Chapter Four

Bink arrived back home in August 2003 in plenty of time to see his baby arrive. Simone threw him a welcome home bash at their new home.

Fox came with his wife and kids, Sidney was there with his wife and kids. I was there with a lady I'd met at Picasso's, one of the many clubs in Virginia Beach.

I wasn't a club person, but this one night I wanted to go out. I jumped in my new 350Z and started roaming through Norfolk, but I ended up on Newtown Road in the Beach. Actually this club was off-limits to active-duty military, or should I say Navy personnel, because of all the shit that kicked off and several Navy boys had lost their lives. So it sounded like somewhere I wanted to hang. Plus, they allowed me in the club with my green-and-yellow Air Force Ones.

Ree-Ree was right there talking to her team when I walked in. I caught her eye. The Stash House jeans and

the green polo with the yellow polo man comple-
mented my sneakers well.

She looked at the Breitling on my left arm, along
with the 1.5-carat white gold pinky ring. The $3,000
bracelet put the icing on the cake. She didn't see a military man, nor a Marine. She thought she saw a hustler.

But I was just a soldier who'd been in training and
letting his money stack. My bonus for signing up was
$10,000, which I'd never spent and the checks I re-
ceived while at Parris Island, in school I saved. And
while training to become the most elite soldier possible, the military fed me, housed me, clothed me and
gave me all my medical and dental free. Then when I
went to Afghanistan, I got extra money for hazardous
conditions, and my money wasn't taxed. I came home
to almost $40,000 in my direct deposit account at Bank
of America.

I brought me a black 350Z and a ZX-10 Kawasaki
Ninja, the fastest bike on the street at the time, espe-
cially when I put my Stage 3 Jet Kit on it and my
Muzzy pipes, shaved the carburetor, timing advancer,
K&N filter, and she was ready.

Then, for my greatest satisfaction, I bought me a
town house with a garage and didn't spend $15,000. I
put $5,000 down on the Z, and $5,000 down on the
bike. And with a VA loan on my house, it was zero
down. My sellers paid my closing costs, so I moved in
without a dime, and was able to treat myself to some
clothes and jewelry.

I knew what I had and what I had to offer, knowing I
was the baddest motherfucker in the club and couldn't
nobody fuck with me, which gave me a certain confidence and shine.

"Want a drink," I said to her, and motioning my head for her to follow me to the bar.

She couldn't hear me, but she read my lips. She walked over to the bar and ordered.

"And I'll take a double Hennessy straight and a Heineken," I said, ordering my drink.

"So what's your name?" She looked at me up and down.

"Bigg. And yours?"

"Ree-Ree," she said slowly.

"Here's your Long Island and double Hennessy," the bartender said, interrupting us and passing me my Heineken.

Then holding her hand out, I pulled out $600 in fifties and twenties, and I saw her eyes flow over the knot that disappeared as fast as it appeared after pulling off the tab and tip.

"Well, come talk to me for a sec," I said, easing from the crowd.

We stepped to where the music wasn't so loud.

"So, Ree-Ree, where you from?"

"Norfolk, Poplar Hall. I went to Booker T. And you?"

"Bayside," I said, smiling.

"You sound like you from down South."

"That's that Carolina in me, but I finished school up here," I said to her.

"Ooh. What you do?"

"I work real hard. Real hard." I smiled.

"Right," she said with a smirk, as if she didn't believe me.

I stared at her for a sec. Her skin was smooth and dark and her eyes so bright, and she had thick, long, black hair that parted down the middle and hung on her back and shoulders. Her size eight frame filled the pink Juicy Couture sweat suit out, but the new pink-and-white Nike Air Max on her size six feet just set off the outfit and made the entire package cute, making you want to take some time and give to her.

"You are beautiful. You have an exotic look. Are you all black?" I asked, knowing she was mixed with something.

"My dad's Dominican, but he not here. He's in the Dominican Republic. That's funny, because a lot of people don't catch it."

"I'm feeling you, baby. Do you club a lot?"

"No!" she answered, sounding offended.

"My bad." I put my hand up, as if to say don't hit me.

She smiled. "I didn't mean it like that. My boyfriend didn't like me to go out. I was with him for four years, so I didn't. We broke up three months ago, and I been in the house. My cousin and friends pulled me out two weeks ago, and we came here, and I had fun. So we came back. I'm enjoying myself," she said, as if trying to convince me that it was all right she was out.

"Look, I'm not pressed to be in the club. And I'm glad I came out and met you. I want to get your number now because, after my drink, I'm out. But what would really make my night is if you go over there and tell your friends you met a nice guy that feels we should get in his new Wrangler with the top off and cruise down the boulevard to Waterside and go walk, talk, and look over the Elizabeth River and see if we think alike. You know what they say. Some people come in your life for a minute, some come for a reason." I gave her a slight smile.

"I think it's *for a lifetime* or something. I'm not sure," she said, shaking her head, "but it's not that."

"Can I try and be smooth? Can I put my words together? Can I try and be a poet or something?" I smiled.

"Yeah, maybe you'll write a book," she said laughing.

"Picture that shit, baby, picture that," I said, getting a little hype as the Hennessy began to take effect.

Ree-Ree laughed.

I watched this gorgeous 5-5 beauty with the posterior that made me shiver walk over to her team. I downed the Hennessy and chased it with the Heineken.

Moments later she waved me over.

I walked up and stood beside her, and she introduced me. Only one among them stood out, and that was her cousin.

"What's your name again?" Barbeda asked.

"Bigg," I said.

"Bigg, my cousin going with you?"

"Yeah, I guess so," I said, tapping Ree-Ree.

"What you do, Bigg? For real? You look like a cool-ass nigga who getting it, so it don't matter, but I don't want my cousin in no shit. Thank you!"

The looks on the faces of Barbeda's friends suggested she wasn't playing.

"I'm a Marine," I said proudly.

"No, you not," one of Barbeda's friends said. "Marines can't have beards. My brother in the Marines."

"I'm on leave right now."

"Know what? Marines is crazy. Ree-Ree, you know Marines is crazy as fuck, girl. Our brother, Chip, he in the Marines." Barbeda looked at her cousin. "And you know he dumped Shara on her goddamn head then went and sat in the chair, lit a cigarette, and drank a beer while that bitch lay crying on the floor with a concussion. I don't know, Ree-Ree," Barbeda said, looking at me. "Call my phone, Bigg, so I'll have your number."

I did that, and me and Ree were out. We rode, we walked, we ate, and she stayed with me.

We slept across my new bed, in my new house. Nothing happened, but after being out there pounding the ground for so long, it felt more than great to have the warmth of a woman, something I truly wanted, and we been going ever since.

My tours and operations had been a strain, but she was still all I wanted, so we worked.

We all gathered around the table with our hands joined as I blessed the food that sat on the table we surrounded. Our heads still bowed, I prayed that He bring Rob back home safe as He had done with us each and every time.

And we said, "Amen."

"Whoa! I thought you was gonna get like your momma," Sidney said.

He along with everybody else started laughing. They all knew my mom. All of us had taken our wives or girls to church when our moms had all come together at one time or another.

Simone was making Bink's plate, as Joy made Fox's. Me and Ree-Ree was getting our stuff on one plate, since we had eaten a lot while making it.

I noticed Sidney and his wife were distant. I knew Sidney, and I felt something. His house was the only house where my mom let me spend the night.

After we ate and talked a bit, the men moved to Bink's room over the garage, where he had a refrigerator with cold beer, and a bar.

"You got an open bar over here, soldier?" Fox poured a drink.

"So how you feeling, Bink?" I asked.

Fox and Sidney looked over at him.

"Man, I'm fine. Just glad to be home."

"That's good to hear," Sidney said.

"It took a minute," I said. "That's why I asked. That's some shit you got to take serious."

"Man, that man all right," Fox said. "He ain't do shit. He ain't see no action. And I made sure shit was right over here, so his job would be easy. Right, soldier?"

"At least he went over and did his part, while the high-paid private sat around Fort Bragg, keeping it safe from the Cross Creek boys," Sidney said.

We all laughed, including Bink.

"It was stressful being over there, but I didn't see a lot of action. The unit Rob with, he got on full body gear all day, locked and loaded."

I went into a deep stare, my mind drifting back to Afghanistan, as Sidney and Fox kept drinking and talking shit. I was well aware that Sidney had been in longer than me. He had all the training I had, except for the diving, but made up for it in his hand-to-hand. Our moms started us together in karate when we were young, but since Sidney had joined 82nd Airborne Division, he'd been sent to Korea, where he studied martial arts. When he got stationed in Japan, he was used as an MP (Military Police), because they couldn't carry guns, only nightsticks, so his skills were not only intimidating, but crucial.

"Y'all know I'm outta here right?" Fox asked, breaking my concentration.

"Where you going?" Bink was ready to hear the news finally, especially since he worked for Fox.

"D.C.," he said.

"I heard that. You should have a ball up there. Got to have a chill job," I said.

"Doing nothing," Sidney added seriously.

"Tripling yo' shit, while you do something, muthafucka," Fox said to Sidney. "Now sit yo' ass down somewhere, before I make you go clean the squad bay or something."

Fox was always pushing shit when he got drunk, but we all knew him.

"You need to slow down," Sidney told him. "You already got two DUIs, and steady fuckin' up."

"My wife downstairs, and she got the keys."

"With two DUIs, you don't need to be drinking at all. You need to be in AA." I laughed.

Bink, who hardly ever really voiced his opinion, said, "He fuckin' up his career. You in a position we all wished we were in, and you drinking it away."

"So how is home life, fellows?" Sidney asked. "Making babies, enjoying the married life?"

"Always so great. Always. Y'all know I gots the finest woman," Fox said.

"Shit! You got the *phattest* woman," Bink said. "Bigg got the finest bitch."

"That ain't his wife," Sidney added. "She ain't really his; she on loan."

Bink told him, "Your woman is your wife, and she still a loan."

We all started laughing.

Sidney actually got mad and walked out. It seemed

his marital problems were worse than I thought, after sitting around and listening to Bink go on and on about him and his wife being married strangers. He said that since Sidney been home, it was as if they didn't really know each other. She was uncomfortable with him touching her, even when they made love.

And the thing that really made us concerned was, they'd only been together five times in three months. We thought it was the pregnancy, but Sidney felt her love had changed.

We drank and tried to forget all the negative—the marital problems, the war, the life changes that weren't good.

I went over and poured five shots for me, Fox, Sidney, Bink, and Rob. We all held up our glasses, and they yelled, "To eighty-second."

I simply said, *"Semper Fi*, soldiers," and we all downed our shots.

"Who turn is it?" Bink asked.

"It's Bigg turn." Sidney handed me Rob's shot.

"For the soldiers who ain't here," Fox said loudly as I downed it.

Every time we were together, we always poured five shots. Somebody had to take the shot or shots for the absent soldiers.

Fox's wife was came upstairs and told him they had to get the kids from the sitter, so they got ready to go. That was like the cue for us all because, when we walked out, our ladies began picking up their purses, giving their hugs and saying good-byes.

We all laughed, joked, and said our good-byes all the way out the door and into the street. It was hard for us to say good night. We had been boys for a lifetime, and being together didn't happen a lot these days.

Chapter Five

On September 13, 2003, I was shipped out to Iraq with the 1 Marine Expeditionary Force (pronounced *first*). We covered a lot of ground, but quite a bit of combat and surveillance was done in the city. The 150-degree heat that came from being on the asphalt slowed down soldiers and Marines, so we were glad to see nightfall, preferring to handle the cold.

I called my mom after being in Iraq for a month. I found out that Sidney and Bink had gotten orders to go to Baghdad.

In January, Bink was inside the chow hall when I got word from Red Cross to call home. It scared the hell out of him. He thought something had happened to his family, but it was Fox. He had been hit with manslaughter charges after getting into a serious accident with one of his kids in the car, and the child died. Fox was drunk at the time.

None of us had seen Fox since he got his orders for D.C. at the end of August. He ended up getting a dishonorable discharge, but the colonel he was assigned to had befriended him. When Fox was going through his entire ordeal, the colonel stood by him then made him a job offer, which he couldn't help but take. At the time Fox's life, his home life, and everything in between was fucked up, and he didn't know which way to turn.

By March 2004, I was headed back home. This tour wasn't as bad as the last, maybe because we didn't lose as many. This time we were better prepared. Soldiers before us knew the land, making us better equipped to handle situations, so there weren't too many surprises.

By the end of April 2004, all 82nd forces in Iraq were redeployed to Fort Bragg, NC, the first time in two years all division units were at Bragg.

I waited for my friends' return. In the last two months, I had gotten my DD 214, so the military was a thing of the past. I had a little change to carry me, but I needed to find a job if me, Ree, and our little boy was gonna be all right.

Rob's time was up also. When he came home, he didn't want any part of the military or Fort Bragg. He left and went to Columbia, SC, where he found a job coaching football, his favorite sport.

My mom had called me to let me know that I needed to holler at Sidney. I knew he had some issues. But since he had just gotten home, I figured there was too much loving and sex going on for him and his wife to be fussing and arguing. His wife had found out that he'd had another baby in Turkey almost the same age as their son. She had found that out when he was home last time, and he didn't say shit. But now she threatening to leave his ass, he was literally crying to his momma, talking about he couldn't take it, and out of all the things in the world, her leaving and taking his boys would be the only thing that would kill him.

After sitting down with my childhood friend, I realized it was no use. He was in a world of his own and was gonna deal with it in a way he saw fit for him, to have peace of mind. I could see the hurt and confusion in my boy, but there was nothing I could say or do.

One of the last times we would come together as soldiers was the end of May 2004, Memorial Day weekend. This week was a race from the start. I had met with Fox three weeks earlier when he had come down to Fort Eustis on some business. When we met, he was driving a new S500 Mercedes Benz.

"What year is this?" I asked. This car was beautiful.

"Two thousand five," he responded with a half-smile.

"Driving an *o* five in *o* four, not a regular car, but top-of-the-line exotic shit. I hear you. So I guess you living all right as a civilian." I laughed.

He smiled, and we gave each other a pound. He gave me a rundown on the business he was into and laid out a plan for me, Rob, Sidney, and Bink to make money. Real money. None of us was seeing no real money.

Actually I was living off savings, which was going fast with a mortgage, Jeep note, bike payment, bills, and Ree-Ree, so when I talked with him, they said we would meet Memorial Day weekend and make it a big thing that Friday.

Saturday was already planned out. That was my family reunion. They always had a big cookout in the country, with a pig spinning on a pole, fried fish, and everything else you could think of. And every woman in Plymouth, NC could cook. I wasn't missing it, and my dad didn't play that anyway. He wanted his kids there. He was really proud of us, and we of him.

On Friday I got up and hooked my bike up to my Jeep and headed out. I left Virginia Beach headed to Fort Bragg. Ree-Ree had left my son with her mom. She knew I was going to meet my boys for a meeting at Bragg and that my family reunion was Saturday in Plymouth, NC. She had been there before, but the mosquitoes ate her ass up so bad, she was never pressed to go back. But when she saw me hook the bike up to the Jeep, she jumped on the phone.

"You out your mind, Bigg. You going to Myrtle Beach for Bikefest? I don't know how you gonna do it, but you gonna do it with me," she said, packing her bag.

"Better hurry up before you get left. My cousins waiting for me in Suffolk," I said, like I had an attitude.

"Should I bring these?" Ree-Ree held up some little-ass jean shorts. "And I'll put this on and leave them unbuttoned," she added, holding a yellow thong in her other hand.

"Girl, you crazy. All your ass be hanging out on the back of the bike. Hell yeah! Bring 'em," I said smiling.

She grabbed her shit, and we were out.

I stopped at my parents' on the way out. Dad was out front, cleaning his shiny burgundy 2003 Gold Wing, which sparkled from front to back and had enough chrome and lights to blind you.

"That's where you get it from," Ree-Ree said.

"And you know it," I said, parking behind his bike getting out the Jeep. "What's up, man?" I asked.

"Take them dark shades off, so I can see your eyes,"

he said, standing up straight. "Nothing much. What's up with you? Headed out?" He continued to wipe his bike after I took off my shades.

"Yes, sir. Going to Bragg then Myrtle Beach, and in Plymouth Saturday by six and church Sunday morning."

"Don't get down there and don't want to leave," he said.

"I know. But I'm coming. Check you later, man." I gave my dad an unusual pound and a hug, ran inside and yelled at my mom, and came back out.

"Be careful, Bigg," he said, watching me leave.

I called my cousins to see if they were still meeting me, but they straight up told me their money wasn't right to flow out of town. I understood and kept it going.

When we got there, the cookout was in full effect at Sidney's momma's house.

I came in and joined my friends. We ate, talked, and had a nice time. Then we went and talked in the corner of the backyard.

As Fox talked with Rob and Bink, I listened carefully. Sidney just stared at me. After Rob and Bink agreed, Sidney looked at me and asked me seriously what was up and was I with that shit. He seemed disappointed in my answer, but he agreed because I did.

The evening was coming to an end, and I had some driving ahead of me. I needed to make a move.

Fox poured five shots of Jose Cuervo 1800. We all held up our glasses, and they yelled, "Eighty-second."

I said proudly, "*Semper Fi.*"

We walked back inside to our significant others. Sidney's mom, Bink's mom, and several other sisters and their kids we grew up with were at the house. As we began to say our good-byes and hit the road, Sidney's mom wanted to pray. We always united by linking hands and bowing our heads as she gave a gracious prayer thanking God for bringing us all home and together again.

After she was done praying, we all said, "Amen."

Just then, something happened that brought tears to dry eyes.

Bink's sister, who was in the Army and stationed in Fort Benning, Georgia, had just got orders to go to Baqubah. She was scared. All she kept saying was, "This is not what I signed up for. I just wanted to get money for school." And she cried.

Then one of the sisters began to sing a song I had never heard.

If we never, pass this way again,
Let's remember this time, and how good it's been
Let's not forget God who made it possible
Just remember He's so wonderful

She sang this over and over until everyone in the room was singing. Some were crying and hugging.

We all walked outside and got another drink for 82nd. Me and Ree-Ree got in the Jeep and headed out, pulling my ZX-10 Kawasaki. I was feeling good, and the night air had me amped. We saw the sign, Interstate 95, 1 mile.

I looked at Ree-Ree, and she looked at me.

"What?" I said.

"It's on you. You driving," she said with an I-don't-care attitude.

"Tell me something."

"Ninety-five *S* Myrtle Beach, ninety-five *N* Virginia Beach, Afr'Am Fest," she said.

"Afr'Am Fest is this weekend," I said, realizing that one of the biggest black events to hit Norfolk was this weekend. "So breakfast and Afr'Am tomorrow then Plymouth an hour and a half away." I turned on 95N.

We got home about one a.m. At first I was hype, but as I entered Virginia a little after twelve, I had a nauseous feeling, so we went straight home. Ree-Ree was 'sleep anyway.

I pulled the bike in the back and went inside. I reached over and called my mom.

"Hello," she answered still half-'sleep.

"I'm back here. I ain't good down there," I said.

"Good, good! I was praying you wouldn't go. I just didn't feel good this time. Usually I don't say nothing, but this time, boy, I said, 'God let him come back.' Boy, I know what you do on that thing. You don't care, you crazy," she said, laughing and waking up.

I laughed too, 'cause she was right. I was gonna do down there and act the fool, make that Ninja scream.

"See, I worry about you. You ain't a safe rider like your daddy," she said, a smile in her voice.

"Where is he? Riding?"

"Naw. He rode to Plymouth earlier this evening. He was gonna help John Lee set up everything. Guess I'll ride with you tomorrow," she said.

"All right. Probably leave about two."

"Okay, baby. Good night, and I love you, boy," she said in a way that I knew her love was genuine.

"Love you too, Ma. Later."

* * *

The ringing of the phone disturbed my sleep.

Looking at the clock, I reached over and answered, "It's seven thirty. What?"

"Get over here, Bigg," my mom said. "The police over here. Hurry up. Please, hurry up."

I jumped up and threw on my shit and flew out the door, shoes untied, pants unbuckled, and rocking only a wife-beater. I jumped in my Jeep and flew down Baker Road, wondering what the police were upsetting my momma for. I didn't give a fuck. Police or not, I was ready to snatch a hole in a motherfucker.

I pulled up and saw the police car in front. I parked and jumped out, and walked in the house. My mom was standing there, tears in her eyes.

"What's going on?" I asked.

"We wanted you here with your mom," the Virginia Beach police officer said. He looked at the other officer and pulled out a card. He read, "Sorry to inform you, but your husband, Edward E. McNair was in a motorcycle accident this morning at twelve twenty-one a.m. on Route 301 in Wilson, NC. He was pronounced dead at twelve forty-three."

The words hadn't come out his mouth good, before my mother let out a deafening scream that crushed my heart as she fell into my arms. I held her real tight, not believing what I'd just heard. I walked her over to the living room couch and sat her down.

The police officers showed their sympathy and made an exit.

My heart was damaged, and I felt like I could break down, but I had to be strong for my mom, hold it together, like my dad would have been.

Still not believing this news, I called to Plymouth to

John Lee's house. "Uncle John, when my daddy leave there?" I asked, tears in my eyes and rattling in my throat.

"He left here last night about ten thirty or eleven. Said he was going to Fort Bragg to catch up with you, so y'all could ride to Myrtle Beach."

My mouth fell open, and tears dripped down my face. I couldn't breathe normally. I had never felt a pain in my chest and gut that wouldn't let up.

My mom took the phone and told John Lee that my dad was dead. John Lee fell to the floor. He had raised my dad and was like a father to him.

His brother Jimmy grabbed the phone. "Shack, Earl dead," Jimmy, aka Shack to most, told the rest of the family. "Crashed on that bike."

I got myself together and got the phone. I needed answers. I called down to Wilson, NC and got one of the officers on the phone that was at the scene. I needed to know what happened.

"Well, sir," she said, "your father was traveling down Route 301, headed north on a two-lane highway, and a drunk truck driver who'd been drinking in a bar across the highway was trying to make it back to his truck and he walked right out into the highway in front of a Honda Gold Wing. The driver of the motorcycle was thrown over the fern and cut open, and then he hit the ground headfirst and instantly broke his neck. If you want more, you, as the family, can request a report."

"Thank you. Ooh, ma'am, before you hang up, what happened to the drunk? Is he hurt?" I was bothered by this man who'd killed my dad.

"He's dead also. He was killed by the impact."

"Thank you again," I said with a smirk.

The pain in my heart dropped a notch. I didn't know why, but it did.

I sat thinking about all I'd been through, the places I'd been, and the things I'd seen. I'd always had a sense of security. The day my dad died, my safety net disappeared, and life got a lot more serious.

Chapter Six

Wednesday, April 20^{th,} 2005

I stood staring down at my longtime friend lying in the beautifully carved casket. Sergeant Lloyd, known to most as Bink, had survived Beirut, Desert Storm, and the bullshit in Iraq, but now all that was left of his life was the flag the military gave his wife.

I stood holding the hand of Bink's wife. I removed my eyes from the body and focused on Sid. Then Rob. Fox stood with his wife as his eyes gazed his surroundings.

As the 21-gun salute rang out, we all stared at each other at the sound of every shot, none of us ever blinking, none of us ever scared. The most cautious, well-trained, disciplined soldiers you'd ever find out here playing these street games, we'd been through hell and back.

The flag was presented to his wife. We watched as she cried hysterically and her friends hugged her for comfort. She slowly walked toward the limo. Fox walked up and touched her arm and escorted her, and I followed, as did Sidney.

Rob walked slowly behind us and said loud enough for me and Sid to hear, "Fake-ass bitch."

Sidney glared at him. "Chill. Not here, not today."

Rob got quiet.

I said nothing, and we continued the slow walk.

Fox and his wife, tears running down their face, stood close to Rhonda as she held the flag tight. It was only weeks ago that their son had died.

We arrived back at the extravagant five-bedroom, two-story home that Bink had built for Rhonda and their three kids. We stood outside talking, trying to figure out how this went down. This was never supposed to happen to Bink, who was doing his last six months. We all had signed for four years, except Capt. Fox.

"What the fuck happen?" Fox walked up with a drink.

We stared at him.

"Stupid muthafuckas can't hear?" Fox asked. He was known for coming off wrong sometimes.

"Fuck you! You still drinking, even after . . ." Sid stopped and frowned at him, trying not to bring up the painful past.

"After what? After what, muthafucka?" Fox said, stepping up on Sid. "Watch your mouth, staff sergeant."

Sid stood firm and blew smoke in Fox's face. "I've destroyed and killed men all over the world. Don't make your bitch get the next muthafuckin' flag," he said real calm.

Fox stared down at Sidney. We all knew if he hit Sidney, he would probably knock his ass out, but we also knew that if he didn't drop him, his wife would receive a flag.

Sidney had outdone all of us and our dads; he was part of an elite group in the Army called Delta Force. Most of the time his location was unknown, and though he never looked like he was in the military, he was one of the most dangerous men in the world. He'd killed many before, and it didn't seem to be an issue.

"Yo! I never got the story. What really happened?" I asked.

"Bink was supposed to be out in the field for two weeks. After four days he got up at two in the morning and ran damn near fifteen miles home in fatigues and boots. Rhonda had dude in the house. Bink and dude got to scuffling, all the way out the door, when dude pulled out the burner and shot him four times," Rob said.

"Who is this nigga?" I asked.

"One of the niggas Bink was dealing with," Sidney said.

"Damn! Y'all can't handle y'all niggas?" Fox asked. "You down here with this nigga, and y'all can't handle your shit."

Fox was head of this shit. Stationed in D.C. at the time of his discharge, he'd met many people during his tour and had befriended a retired lieutenant colonel who ran a business that caused him to run in and out of the country. Fox was never stopped, and his duffel bags were never checked.

Fox and his colonel friend made a lot of money on the streets of D.C., so when we saw how he was living, we never knew. He set Rob up in Columbia, SC. Fox had peoples down there, so Rob began running to SC and eventually moved.

Bink was to stay in "Fayettenam" with Sidney.

I was in the Southeastern district of Virginia, Virginia Beach, to be exact. While there, I met some Navy niggas that loved to sniff. I used to fuck around with it too, so we hung strong. The same shit Fox had, I had seen many Navy boys, myself, and other Marines spend most of our check on, getting high.

I fell in love with Tidewater, so I moved back to Virginia Beach to serve these boat boys and military officers that Fox hooked me up with. Now we were all in different states, but we were there for each other, and we made money.

"How the fuck we gonna handle this?" Rob asked. "I got to get back to Columbia. I told him to leave that sorry bitch. She been trifling since her ass was at Pine Forest."

"You gonna take this shit, Rob," Fox said, "and you gonna have some extra in your pack, Bigg."

"Fuck that! I ain't doing shit," I said. "I'm out. I just need to know about the dude who killed Bink."

"You right," Fox said. "They have to have his funeral."

"They will, when they find him," Sidney said with a smirk.

We all smiled, knowing that mission had already been completed. We said our good-byes and headed home.

Rob knew he was gonna have to hit the road and do some work in Fayetteville, and I also knew my package was gonna be extra heavy and nothing could be done. I was driving up 95, thinking about Bink and how he lost his life to a nigga who was fucking his wife. This was supposed to be the one woman that he knew was his, and he might get a nigga for fucking with her, never thinking the nigga was gonna fuck him twice, first his wife, and second with his life. I thought married life was supposed to be a safe haven.

My mind went into deep thought as I traveled back to Virginia Beach. I leaned over and grabbed the pack of Backwoods on the seat and pulled out one of the already rolled L's from out the pack. I eased into a state of relaxation as the haze-filled Backwoods filled the new S550.

I was running about 80, so Fox had to be doing 90 in front of me in the new Chrysler 300. He was on his way back to D.C. I blew at him as I turned on to Highway 58, headed to Tidewater.

My heart was touched as I thought about me, Bink, Fox, Rob, and Sidney walking to Leigh Field House to swim, or going to the gym, all on the base. Kids having fun, not worried about nothing. Now Fox was married with kids of his own, Rob had had one kid while at Fort Bragg.

I had a four-year-old son in Norfolk with some sexy-ass girl from Norfolk. Met her ass at the club, should have left her there, but I took her home, and she ended up staying three years before I sent her ass back home.

I thought about the looks in each other's eyes as we all went our separate ways to separate cities, like we were never gonna see each other again. Death had never touched this close. Bink never saw 23, Fox was 24, Rob was 23, and Sidney was 25, two years older than me.

Rob said his good-byes as he climbed in the Navigator and pulled off. He was 6 ft, 310 pounds, and looked as if he would destroy a nigga, but he was mad nice. Never wanted drama. Fox stood 6 ft also, but was only 200 lbs. He was that slim cat, always talking slick and would get some shit going. Then he would disappear. He was married and spent most of his time with his family.

I was only 5-8, 230, worked out and knew my body was a temple. I wanted to continue to look good.

I'd been classified as being bipolar because sometimes I changed without reason, and I didn't talk much to people I didn't know.

I looked at Sidney as Fox said his last words to him through the window and pulled off. I slowed down and gave him a firm grip. I stared into his eyes, and the grip got tighter. He had a cold stare in his eyes.

"I love you, man," I said. "You know where I'm at, and you got a key."

"I know, Bigg, I know," Sidney said, without emotion.

I pulled off as he got into a 95 Ford Mustang, an old car that wasn't in his name. He didn't have an address and was the only one in the crew without a cell phone. This cat didn't exist.

Me and Sidney went way back, to babies in a crib. Sidney's mom and my mom were sisters in Christ. Rob, Fox, and Bink came along when we were like six or seven. Our dads were 82nd Airborne and used to go out drinking, fighting, and acting the fool before coming home fucked up. Our moms spent a lot of time together in church, prayer meetings, and revivals. We were in church four to five nights a week, and me and him were tight as thieves, so I understood him like no other. And we trusted each other like brothers, with a love that nobody could ever infiltrate.

I thought back to not quite a year ago when I got a call at five in the morning from Bink. He told me that

Sidney was in trouble. He'd just seen it on the news. A family was murdered in Corregidor Courts, base housing on Bragg. Somebody broke in at three in the morning and killed Sidney's wife and two kids. There was so much blood on the walls and in the bedrooms, they boarded the house up for two years.

Sidney was picked up and charged with the bloodiest homicide ever in the city of Fayetteville. His alibi was, he was in the field, twenty miles away. Strange fingerprints were in the house, and neighbors said that his wife was seeing some man secretly. All the same, they held him until the trial began.

Sidney had talked to me a month earlier, after he had come to Newport News. We met in Hampton at Crabbers, and over drinks, he told of his wife's cheating, and that his two sons knew the man. I remember him telling me it would be easier to deal with death than her taking his boys and leaving.

During the trial, he cried and begged the jury to believe he could never hurt his family. They found it impossible for him to run home, kill a family, and run twenty miles back in a night.

I finally got a second alone with Sidney. He talked real quick about missing his family. He was all alone and he let his head fall on my shoulder and in a low tone and a different voice, he said, "I run twenty-eight miles with a forty-pound ALICE pack on my back. Wonder how fast it can be done without it? No mistakes, Bigg, no mistakes." Then he began to cry.

I stood in shock. I knew he was cold, but a man who could do this wasn't to be fucked with. But this was my friend, and I had nothing but love for him.

*   *   *

I slowed down as I made my way through Emporia knowing this city made mad money off out-of-towners speeding. After doing 60 for about forty-five minutes, I was glad to see the "Welcome to Suffolk" sign. I increased the speed to 75, until I got on 64, where I let her ass sit on 90.

I was now approaching Virginia Beach, the city I was now calling home. Coming from Carolina, I never thought niggas could be so different. These VA cats were in a class separate from us, and not like New York niggas. Their hustle was different, their game was different, and their outlook on life was different.

I was quickly influenced after meeting my baby momma. I was taking care of this girl, and niggas kept saying no, but I was in love. She took my Southern hospitality for weakness, and we later went separate ways.

Because I was in the military, she thought I was a brother who wanted something out of life and would do no wrong, never realizing that I came from a house that was run by strict military rules—"Yes, ma'am! No, ma'am! Yes, sir! No, sir!" And my dad never spared the rod, and I mean never. Nor did he ever stand for anybody challenging him. And the way he would come home fucked up off that Johnny Walker Red and would go to my mother's ass, if we were up, and only if we were up, he did beat our ass.

So I became a true believer that if your woman got out of line, you had the right to beat her ass and her kids. She kept taking me wrong, until my dad came out of me, the side that came home from Grenada. The side I'd seen grab my mother by the throat and squeeze it until she would be staring into space and then fall to her knees. He would have a crazy look in his eyes, as her eyes bulged, and tears would roll from the corners of her eyes, as her mouth formed an *O* and she fought for air, her hands would grip his forearm, but did little, because her 5-2, 118-lb. frame was no match for the former 82nd Airborne First Sergeant.

I would yell, "Dad, please! Dad, please!"

He would shake his head.

Then I would yell, "First Sergeant! First Sergeant, stand down!" and he would snap to attention, letting her go.

I felt his wrath later in life. I too found out that his grip was unbreakable, and all you could do was pray.

I remember the night my girl pushed that button and came in my house at quarter to five in the morning. The house was dim. She never saw me coming as I leaped for her throat and began squeezing, thoughts of her laying with another man running through my mind. I was somebody else, and my mind was somewhere else. She fought and grabbed at my arm, but her body began to calm.

When I snapped back, she had fallen to her knees. Her beautiful soft eyes that made me melt now bulged out her face, and tears ran from the corner of her eyes. Her mouth was in the shape of an *O*, while she gasped and fought for air. I stared at her and saw my mother. Even though I knew I was wrong at that point, my hand kept tightening as she fell back against the wall lifeless.

I went to the couch and sat down, rolled an *L*, and tried to figure out what I was going to do with her body if she was dead, at the same time hoping and praying she wasn't.

When she came to, she got all her shit, walked outside, and saw the cab. Then she realized her key to my car and house were gone, she tried to scream, but her emotions got her.

"I hate you, Bigg," she tried to yell. "Why you take my car?" She leaned over to get her bag. Her hands shook, and her face was turning dark, darker than her regular complexion. The tears ran down her cheeks as she tried to pull the bag.

I actually wanted to help her. "Let whoever yo' ass was with last night buy you a car and give you a key, trifling bitch!" I said, not realizing how fast it came out.

The cab driver got out and helped her put her bag in the trunk.

She stared at me as she opened the door to the cab. She wiped the tears that wouldn't stop. "I never thought you would do this to me!" she cried.

"Get the fuck out of here before the coroner has to carry you away from here," I said.

She'd brought this shit on herself, and it still was eating me up. I wanted to stop, grab her, and start over, but inside I knew I was done. I was really done.

I pulled in my garage. The ride from Emporia to home had exhausted me, but I had people to see and money to get. I went to the drawer and retrieved my work phone. I had thirty-seven missed calls, thirty from my baby moms. I called her back.

"Where you been, Bigg?" she screamed.

"My moms in Carolina. What the fuck you want?"

"Your son laying in intensive care down in Norfolk General," she said with frustration.

"What? What the fuck happen?"

"He was playing outside, and some bitch lost control

of her car and came on the curb. Hit LB and Li'l
Keisha. Me and Keisha was inside talking."

"You weren't watching him?" I yelled. I knew it wasn't
her fault, but somebody had to take the blame.

"Bigg, shut up!" she yelled. "Li'l Keisha died, and
Li'l Bigg need you."

"On my way!"

I had to get to my son quickly. I opened the garage,
grabbed my helmet, and pulled out my 2005 ZX-10
Kawasaki. In minutes I was on the interstate running
110 mph down 264. I had Li'l Bigg racing through my
mind. I couldn't lose him. I lived for that li'l nigga. My
eyes watered at the thought of losing my son. I quickly
cleared my head, knowing I had better concentrate on
handling this rocket I was sitting on.

As I came up on the exit headed to downtown Norfolk, 264, I hit the curb extremely fast, so I leaned low
as my boot scraped the ground. I brought her down to
fourth gear in the curb, the speedometer reading 80
mph. I looked at the ground. I was so low, I could have
scooped some gravel.

Something came through me, and I tightened my
grip as I straightened up to come out the curb. Two
bikes came into view coming onto the interstate. I
knew this red-and-white Yamaha and all-black 1300
Suzuki Hayabusa. I saw them before they saw me. I
dropped her into third at 85. The front wheel came up,
but I rode it out, never letting up.

By the time she came down, I was at 110 again and
going. My head was low as my speedometer reached
130, and my left mirror showed me a Yamaha light
about forty yards back and stable. My right mirror
showed a bright light coming up fast. I had her wide

open. I was approaching 150 when the Suzuki flew by.
I let up.

They ended up following me to Norfolk General. We
parked and started walking in.

"Who here, cuzzo?" Li'l Nate asked.

"LB. Bitch let him get hurt," I said to him, trying to
get control. "What up, Cat?"

"Chilling, cuz," he said, giving me a pound.

Li'l Nate was my cousin from Plymouth, NC. His
man was from Roper, down the street. Li'l Nate was the
biggest Brooks and the wildest, and meanest, but his
man Cat was a tall, slender, calm, quiet dude. Never
knew why they hung until I put my hand on their
work.

I rushed inside, where my little man was laid up, IV
in his arm, leg up in traction, cast on his body from the
waist down.

"Goddamn, Ree! What the fuck!" I said.

"Calm down, Bigg," Buck said. "It wasn't her fault."
Buck was Ree's new man.

"Fuck you, nigga! That ain't your son."

"Fuck me? Naw, fuck you, nigga! You wasn't even
here for your son."

"Don't get slapped in your muthafuckin' mouth,
boy!" Li'l Nate stared Buck down.

"Y'all country niggas a joke to me, cuz. And you too,
boat boy." Buck smiled at me.

I left shit alone. I knew Li'l Nate and Cat would take
it there, no question, and I knew Buck wasn't gonna
back down.

I didn't know what this nigga did, but three months
after we broke up, Ree-Ree dropped my son off in a
new 745 and let me know it was hers. Then when I

seen her at the club, she was pushing a 2005 Range Rover, which she let me know was Buck's.

Ree-Ree also let me know she didn't need child support. Her and my son was living with Buck in his five-bedroom home with a pool. She had caught her one. I was a little jealous, not because he had all this and her, but he was in love. She had him open, and he treated her like a queen and controlled her ass like I never could.

"Your son needs some blood. Go see the doctor," Ree-Ree said.

I could tell she wanted to hug me. I wanted so bad to grab her for strength, but she knew better. I walked down the hall, gave blood, and went back to the room.

A couple of hours had passed when the nurse came inside and asked to speak to me and Ree-Ree in private.

Buck, Li'l Nate, and Cat, amongst other nurses, came running up as they heard Ree-Ree's screams pierce the hallways. "No! No! No!"

I heard nothing. My heart was heavy and full of so much pain that it took my legs away. I was on the floor, unable to move. I was hurting and wanted to ball up and cry.

Buck grabbed Ree-Ree and pulled her in his arms.

"What's wrong, Ree-Ree?" her man asked as he held her tight.

She squeezed him and continued to cry hysterically.

Li'l Nate and Cat helped me to my feet. I took three deep breaths and regained my composure and stood up straight.

"Yo, man," I said slowly, looking at Buck, "take care of Jamil. Li'l nigga ain't even mine. This bitch got me." I turned and walked away.

"I'm sorry, Bigg, I'm sorry!" she screamed at my back. "I had no idea, Bigg! I really didn't!"

"Calm down, Ree," I heard Buck say. "I love Jamil, and I love you. Let him go."

Ree-Ree hugged Buck tight. She probably figured she'd never find this kind of love nowhere. Buck had her living good. She loved him, but she was in love with me. She opened her eyes and watched as we strolled through the double doors. She knew it was for real. It would be our last encounter.

She dreamed of getting back together, but we both had issues. She knew I was the only nigga who held her heart. I was that Carolina-raised, VA-bred "bird dog." My hustle game was tight, my pimp game was on point, and I had everything Buck had—single family condo with four bedrooms, and a finished room over the garage; new CLS 500 for shine; new 2006 Tahoe; plus my Ninja and my Kawasaki jet ski.

We walked out in silence until we reached the bikes.

"Whoa! My cousin burnt me up coming here. That bitch burned me up leaving. What the fuck am I to do?" I asked seriously.

"What I did is going to happen over and over. Bigg, what she did, only one time." Li'l Nate put his arm around my shoulder. "Now call Aunt Catherine and let her know that she ain't got no real grandson and to save that love for some real Brooks young'uns."

They laughed, but I didn't find anything funny.

I called my mom. She was hurt, but more upset about Jamil. I understood. She went from mom to Evangelist Catherine Brooks. I put her on the speaker. She began to pray as Li'l Nate, Cat, and myself bowed our heads in the parking lot and gave glory to God for all that He'd done and all that He was going to do, like she told us.

When she was finished, we all said, "Amen."

Then it was mom on the phone again. "Tell Li'l Nate momma to call me," she yelled.

"All right, Aunt Cat," he said.

"Hold it down," she said and hung up.

"Ready now, man?" Cat asked. "Moms made me feel better."

"Where to?" I asked.

"Shit! You the nigga with all the money. I got to go tell Momma that my cousin making so much money in VA, he taking care of other muthafuckas' kids," he said, throwing on his helmet.

It was time to have fun. The two Muzzys and the Vance Hines pipe had the parking lot sounding off.

Then we lit up the interstate like there was no to-morrow, like we really didn't care if we lived to see to-morrow. The ride was a stress reliever.

I pulled up to the garage and parked, ran inside, cut off the alarm, and raised the garage. I reached for a soda, I held the can as I stepped down into my den, the picture of Jamil struck me. The one person I'd lived my life for was snatched away. I felt like shit inside, not because Ree-Ree had got me. But I actually wished he had died rather than get the news that he wasn't mine.

I put the soda back and pulled the fifth of Hennessy from the bar, poured a stiff drink, and grabbed a Heine-ken. The more I drank, the more I cried.

I finally stripped down and got in the shower. I real-ized I could cry and the water would camouflage my tears. I stayed in until the water ran cold. I felt empty, like nothing, and I had no love for no one.

My phone was ringing. I had three text messages from Ree-Ree.

Text 1: *I need to see you bad. We have to talk, things can't end like this.*

Text 2: *Please don't leave me when I need you so much. Please Bigg. I love you.*

Text 3: *We don't do this, we talk Bigg. I'm going home to shower and change. I'm stopping by.*

I looked at the message time. Thirty minutes had passed. I threw on my Rocawear sweats and white tee and started texting: *Do Not Come By. Holla another time.*

Before I could set my phone down, it rang.

"I'm outside, open the door," she said.

"Why are you here? Go take care of yours." I really wanted her to leave. I hated her for what she'd done. She fucked me up and confused an innocent child with her bullshit.

"I'm knocking. Open up!" she screamed.

I opened the door, and seeing her made me lose it. "What?" I yelled. "What could you possibly want, trifling bitch?"

"I didn't know, Bigg. Before I started talking to you, I was messing with this married guy, but from the time you started coming over, you were there every day and night, Bigg. I even had a period after that. You know I didn't do this on purpose, Bigg, you know that."

"I don't know shit! Girl, I could kill your ass." I grabbed her by her neck with both hands and slammed her to the couch.

Her eyes widened, and my anger quickly turned back to hurt and pain. I fell in the seat beside her, taking deep breaths, and put my face in my hands, so she couldn't see the tears.

She began hugging me and pushed me back, cradling my head in her arms. "I'm sorry, baby. I'm sorry, baby. I am so sorry. I never meant to hurt you. I love you so much."

She began kissing my forehead, face, cheeks, and hugging me, her kisses going from pampering to affectionate. I thought she was losing it. Did she think sex could cure this? Or did she feel so low that she would do whatever for my forgiveness? She was really confused.

She reached down and slid her hands in my sweats and grabbed my rock-hard dick. She went down and started licking the head and then up and down my dick. Then she started sucking it.

I stared down at her, my hard dick going in and out of her mouth.

"God, I missed you," I whispered. I really didn't miss her, but I did miss this bomb-ass head. "That shit feel so good. Suck it, Ree-Ree. Please don't stop." I was thinking, *This trifling bitch is either crazy or stupid*, but until this hard dick spit, it didn't matter.

"I know you sorry, girl. We gonna work it out. Okay, baby?"

She kept sucking.

"Okay, baby?" I tried to keep from laughing.

"Okay." She went back to sucking.

I stared down at her. Her stupidity was making my dick harder. As I thought about Jamil laying up there hurt, I got madder. I wanted revenge. As I thought about this girl having another man's kid and living with this nigga Buck, I realized I had no connection whatsoever to this trifling, fucked-up-ass girl, who was willing to bow down and try to win my heart, not knowing I had no heart and no love when it came to her. Her sexual openness had the grimiest shit coming out in me.

I turned her over and straddled her face as I pumped in and out her mouth. I grabbed my cell phone and took pictures. Then I grabbed her face, cheeks in each hand and fucked her mouth until my nut exploded and ran from her mouth to her chin. I took my T-shirt off and wiped her face and mouth.

"I'm sorry, baby. I want to be with you, Bigg."

"I know. We gonna work on this. You know you all that to me, but you hurt me. Maybe we can make our baby for real." I hugged her, her head on my stomach. I almost laughed. It was hard keeping it in.

"Get me hard. I'm ready to be inside you."

I threw my dick in her mouth before she could respond, and she sucked just like before.

I lifted her up, pulled down her pants, and began banging. I fucked hard and good then I pulled out and came on her stomach and chest. Wiped her off again, fixed her clothes, and encouraged her to get back before Buck realized she'd been gone too long.

"Oh! And call me. I got to know how my man is doing." I smiled and gave her a hug. "Call me, baby."

She smiled, got in the Range Rover, and drove off.

I went and got another shower, wondering what I had just done.

Chapter Seven

Wednesday, May 18, 2005

"Fuck you! I wish you were dead!" were the first words Fox heard when he walked inside of his eleven-room home outside of Washington, D.C. He decided, since he was running in the streets of D.C., that Alexandria was a better place to live, but what he was going through, his location had nothing to do with it.

"I hate you! I hate you!" Joy yelled, her hands swinging wildly.

Fox grabbed her arms and pushed her to the couch, but she never stopped. The look in his eyes as he tried to restrain her was one of anger and hurt. He was hurt because he'd made a mistake almost a year ago and was still paying for it, and would pay for the rest of his life.

Joy used all her strength trying to get away and began kicking him. He felt himself being overwhelmed by her. She was too much to contain. He tried to get a grip of himself and her, but it was too hard. An open-hand slap with the left hand and two fingers directly to the windpipe made her lose her breath.

That scared her, as she fell to her knees, her hands wrapped around her throat.

He looked into her eyes, and her arms went out for him to help her. But his knees buckled, and he fell to the floor and grabbed her, his eyes swollen with tears as he held her and rubbed her back.

She squeezed him and took deep breaths. "I'm-I'm-I'm so . . ." was all she could get out.

"Don't. Shh! Shh!" Fox rubbed her head and stroked his fingers through her hair. "Don't say a word. Don't say a word. It's all right."

He held her until she fell asleep in his arms. He then picked her up and took her to bed.

Fox walked back downstairs, went to his bar, and closed the bottle of Absolut she'd left open. She'd become a constant drinker since the accident. He poured himself some Hennessy V.S.O.P.

As he took that first swig, he gripped the glass as the bright lights of the train flashed then tore his Escalade to pieces. He never saw it because of his drunkenness at the time, but he'd never forgotten the sight as he turned around and saw his son's body crushed between the metal. It was too much to behold, and he fought to remove the car seat and metal, but it was useless. The metal went deeper into his hands, and his screams got louder and deeper as his little boy shut his eyes.

When the ambulance and police arrived, they pulled him from the truck. His entire ride to the hospital, he wished he'd died, and to this day, he'd still wished he'd died. He was released from the hospital and arrested on three charges, drunk driving, negligence, and manslaughter.

So here he was facing the world and the system that was trying to convict him and lock him up for the death of his son. And he never knew who he was going to come home to, the wife that understood his pain and nightmares, the wife that blamed him and would never let him forget, or the wife that would go into a deep stare, sometimes directly at him, for long periods of time.

He knew he'd made a mistake, and living with it was enough punishment. Nobody knew the pain he felt. Losing a child was one thing, but being the cause of the loss was quite another.

He finished the drink and poured another. He leaned back and pulled out his cell.

"Hello, sir," he said, still giving the colonel his respect.

"What you say, captain?" the colonel responded. "My Benz is at a shop on M Street. Before going into Georgetown, please get that to my office."

"Will do, sir, will do."

Fox hung up and called his friend Erica, who answered instantly.

"Hey, captain."

"Need two girls at one o'clock, okay."

"Gotcha!" she said and hung up.

Erica knew to get two rooms at the Days Inn in one hour. She hit him with the room, and in one hour she was floating the 535 BMW into the city, with Fox on the side leaned back.

Erica was one of the soldiers that worked under him when he was active. She was enlisted personnel, and he knew she was hands-off then. Now it was something that crossed his mind and hers, but nothing was ever said, and no lines were ever crossed. She was about money, and after rolling with him, she was now building her own clientele.

Fox spotted the colonel's 2005 E-Class when Erica made her turn on M. He got out, got in the Benz, and drove off, headed to his townhouse in Arlington.

They reached his spot and pulled in the garage. His man, 1st Lt. Rodriguez, better known as Butch, was already there. Butch was a light-skinned, wavy-haired pretty boy from the south side of Richmond. He had a naturally cut body, and at 6-2, the females fiended for him, especially when he was in uniform.

Butch had hollered at Erica after he'd met her working at the Pentagon. He wasn't supposed to be fraternizing with the enlisted personnel, but he really didn't care. The more they hung out, the more she realized he was an officer and a thug. She knew officers made money, but after chilling with him in his $2,600-a-month three-bedroom condo in the Georgetown section of D.C., and watching him spend money like she thought an officer had, and the many times he would pull his Platinum Card, she thought he was established. But it was the weekend he asked her to go home with him and she decided to go that she experienced what he was really about.

He pulled his 2004 Honda Accord up to the garage of his four-bedroom, two-car-garage home in Chesterfield County, fifteen minutes outside of Richmond.

When she walked into his house, she asked if it was his parents' home. He laughed, walking into his room to change his clothes, throw on jewels, and a fitted cap.

He opened the garage, and she saw the 2006 Range Rover sitting on 22s with legal tint. Beside it was a '92 Cadillac STS on 22s with a candy paint job.

They jumped in the Range.

"What happens at home stays at home," he said to her. "You got me?"

Erica nodded.

Butch filled the car with some haze-rolled Dutches as he cruised Richmond, up and down Broad, from club to club, getting VIP, pulling out stacks of money. In every club, he was shown love, so by the early morning, Erica realized he was "that nigga."

They'd stopped talking after a few months, but became close friends and remained tight. She later introduced Butch to Fox, and it had been on ever since.

They unloaded the Benz without a sound. Butch had the scales set up as they began to break fifteen kilos down for distribution. This was every month, and just like every month, things were on point.

"Sit these three over there for Columbia," Fox said. "And sit these three over there for Tidewater. These three going to Richmond, these three for D.C. Now, these suppose to go to Carolina, but under the circumstances, I got to take one, sending one to Tidewater to Bigg. And only one is going to Bragg,"

"We gotta put in some work," Erica said. "That ain't nuthin'."

Butch sent her a rare smile. "Listen to you, hustler."

Him and Fox laughed.

"My road dog straight," Fox said. "I got her." He stared at her. "Know this."

Erica smiled and began breaking down and packaging what they were going to distribute. They did everything fast and in a military fashion.

Erica broke out, headed to the hotels, Butch to Richmond, and Fox got on the phone to let me and Rob know that them things were headed our way.

Fox knew he had to go back to Fayetteville and make sure things were still correct. He couldn't accept the loss, and fucking with his friends, teaching them the game, he'd been through his share of losses.

Fox arrived back at his home. It was about two a.m. when he walked inside. Joy was sitting in the dark. He turned on the light. The sight of his once beautiful wife was a sight to behold. Darkness surrounded her eyes, and sadness covered her face.

"What you doing?" he asked, standing back staring at her.

At first she ignored him. Then she stood up. "Did you leave our son outside?"

"No, baby, I didn't."

"Where is he?" she screamed.

"I'll get him."

Fox cased the room and gathered a few things. He heard her mumbling in the den, where she was sitting, holding a drink. He strolled back in. Again he just stared.

"How?" she asked.

"What?"

"How are you going to get our son? You know he's gone, and you need to accept that. I really miss him and how things used to be." She sipped her drink.

When Fox eased closer to her, she forced a smile and leaned her head against his chest and rested. He held her and cherished this moment. This was her normal state of mind.

"Shh," she said. "Just hold me. Squeeze me. Let me know that you're by my side . . . that you are forever by my side." She pulled him as close as she could.

He held her, not wanting to let go. They'd been through hell and back, but this was the lady he chose as his wife, and through it all, his love kept coming back strong. He pulled away and looked into her eyes. She stared back, and he could see the hurt, but she was trying to smile.

"I know you have to go handle your business," she said, nodding.

"Just a day. I won't be long."

"I know what you have to do. Take care of your business and get on back. I love you, baby!"

Fox made his exit. He always felt better making moves when he knew his wife was okay. He jumped in his car and pulled out. He stopped and looked at his wife standing in the doorway. She waved as he pulled off in the silver CLK.

Fox grabbed his phone and called Erica. "Everything good?" he asked.

"Yes, sir. And that's on the way. Everything is on schedule and falling in place."

"Good. See you in a couple days."

Fox looked up Rob's number and dialed.

"What up, soldier?"

"Fuck you think?"

"See you in seven," Fox said.

"Yeah. I'm still in Columbia."

Rob was always doing what the fuck he wanted, and that was the minimum, moving his shit in bulk and chilling. So he wasn't trying to hear that Fayetteville shit. Niggas at home wasn't to be trusted.

"I'll be there in seven. You know." Fox hung up. He knew Rob understood.

Once on the 95 South, he lit the Black & Mild and clenched the cigar between his teeth. He leaned back and slid in his new Lyfe Jennings CD. Then he pulled out the pint of Hennessy he had in the armrest and took a big swig. *Life and the pain that comes with it has to get better*, he thought. He took another swig. *It has to.*

Chapter Eight

Wednesday, June 15, 2005

The head coach of Lower Richland finished his final words to the coaching staff. He'd been defensive line coach since moving there. His resume for playing ball in the Army and his tapes of being a beast at Pine Forest, All-State tackle would be something he'd mention to prove any point.

He grabbed his bag and notebook and exited the field house. He reached his truck and tossed his bag in the back. He pumped the sounds of Three 6 Mafia. He loved that down South shit, especially them ATL niggas.

He pulled into his condominium complex, Relax Shores Condo, starting at $200,000, with three and four bedrooms available. They were on their final phase. A year ago he'd bought a three-bedroom that could have been a four out, but he opted for a loft. So his was like a three-story condo with a two-car garage.

He loved his truck, he loved his house, but as he approached his street, he prayed his third love was—

"Yes," he said out loud as he spotted the black 2006 Avalon parked in front of his garage. "Reignah, I love you," he said. "Been on my mind all fuckin day."

He pulled up and hit the switch to the garage. After she pulled in, he pulled in beside her, jumped out the truck, secured the area, then put the garage door down. She stepped out of the Avalon, and just like every day for the past eight months, her eyes and beautiful dark brown complexion with jet-black hair that lay on her shoulders and rested on her back made him happy to have her. And when she smiled, she had him. She was soft as butter.

He hugged her, putting his arms around her small waist as her medium frame fell into his arms, and kissed her, but she pulled away, grabbed his face, and threw her tongue down his throat.

He leaned back and looked at her up and down in her khaki-colored skirt suit. *Damn, she is sexy*, he thought. He could taste the alcohol on her breath. It was Wednesday night, and she'd been out for drinks. Her mouth met his again, and he knew. He pulled her shirt open and reached back and undid her bra and began sucking her breast, while pulling up her skirt. He pulled her already soaked panties to the side and threw his hard, sweaty dick into her as she leaned back on the Avalon.

They gripped each other, realizing the great feeling that came from spontaneous sex. They went for twenty minutes in the garage until they ended up on the back seat of the truck. Then they rested for a few before going inside straight to the shower.

Rob was sitting on his couch rolling a honey Dutch, when she came out of the shower and dropped her towel. Her full breasts, slim waist, and petite ass had him hard again instantly, not to mention her soft, innocent look. She kneeled down and pulled his dick out of the leg of his shorts and began licking the head.

Rob had no choice but to drop the Dutch and let the "Arizona" rest on the table. Fifteen minutes later, she was sprawled out on the bed exhausted.

He went back to his Arizona and Dutch that was on the coffee table sitting in front of the dark brown leather set in the loft. He hit the remote for the CD player. Ciara came blasting through with her remix with Petey Pablo.

"That's my nigga," he yelled. "Rip that shit, Petey. "Greenville nigga, what? Fayettenam nigga." He lit his Dutch. He poured himself a shot of Patrón and took it to the head then poured another and let it sit as he continued to make the Dutch disappear. He picked up the shot glass and downed the smooth tequila. Then he pulled out his NFL Madden and began playing.

It wasn't long before Reignah was up, standing in front of him naked. She poured a shot of Patrón, downed it, and sat next to Rob.

"What we eating?" she asked.

"Whatever. I ain't going nowhere."

"Pizza then," and she went and made the call.

Rob paused the game as she strolled off, just to admire the sexy young woman. And a woman she was. Some would call her a slow-moving, prissy, quiet bitch with attitude, but once he got to know her, she came across as a well-educated, professional young lady.

Rob had dated all kinds of women, from eighteen to thirty, from young girls impressed with his truck sitting on 23's to the single moms of the kids he coached who fell in love with the way he handled their out-of-control boys by just speaking. He was well respected and became like a father figure to many of the young men, and many mothers found that strength attractive and showed their appreciation in many ways.

So, for the last couple years, he hadn't had anything steady until he came across Reignah, and his other options slowly disappeared. He was proud to say that for seven months, two weeks, and one day he had been true. When they'd met, he never thought it would escalate to this. When Travis had introduced him to his cousin, it was because he didn't know his way around Blacksburg, VA.

Rob had coached Travis in high school and had seen him go from a good player to a beast on the field. He saw mad potential in Travis, so by him being defensive coach, he advised him to use a little weight, get faster, and instead of being on all-city tackle, be an all-state linebacker.

Travis came from a good home, where all his needs were met, but what he wanted was another thing. He had a car, a '91 Camry, but he wanted a truck sitting on 23's like Rob. He had white DC's in fair condition and Timbs, but he wanted every color DC to match his different color Rocawear, Enyce, and LRG, like Rob, who had DC's and Timbs in every color.

Rob saw the desire in Travis for football and money, but this wasn't until he saw Travis sprinting across the schoolyard with security on his ass. Travis hit the building corner and tossed the bag, only to see Coach Rob standing there. Rob picked up the bag and put it in his pocket as security ran by.

They eventually caught up with Travis, but Rob got his truck and left. That would be the first time he invited Travis to his house.

"Come on in, Travis," Rob said.

"Coach, I'm sorry, but I need dough," Travis said. "It ain't all about football."

"Yes, it is! Grades and football, money will come."

"I want money now. Fuck that, coach. Not to shine and bring attention like those simple-ass niggas on the team, or those broke-ass cats in the projects, but money to do what I want. Buy clothes, take out girls, get rooms, buy weed. Come on, coach, you ain't that old."

"So you sell cake in school? You run around with drugs in school? Half ounce of coke can end all your shit, and have you locked, nigga. Fuck is wrong with you? How much was that?"

"Six hundred front."

Rob went in his pocket and pulled out a stack. He peeled off a thousand and handed it to Travis.

Travis looked stunned. "What's this for?"

"Pay your man, step away, and depend on me. Between me and you, I'll give you an allowance every week. If I call you, come see me, but nothing on or near the school. NEVER!! You hear me? Listen to me, you'll have money from now til you go pro."

Rob smiled, and they bonded.

Travis shined on and off the field. He began making runs for Rob after practice, and eventually built his own clientele of his peers, with the white girls he was fucking, but he only sold at six in the morning.

Travis was now living the way he wanted to live. On the field he was a beast, and this coke game and hustling game, he felt he had mastered. That's why when he was offered a full scholarship to VA Tech or Miami, Coach Rob was more than a coach, he was a friend, and consulting him was everything.

"After all this time, which one is it?" Rob asked Travis as they stood outside the field house.

"Tech. VA Tech," Travis said slowly.

"That's it. Send me a ticket, I'm there," Rob said, shaking his hand and hugging him. "I'm proud, I'm proud," he added with a laugh. "So you done with the business?"

"Well, I wanted to leave it in the hands of my cousin, but I didn't know if it was cool."

"Your cousin who?"

"Naheem."

"Naheem Alexander is your cousin?"

"Yeah! He the shit, but money come first. Always money."

Rob looked into Travis' eyes. "Naheem is the best back in the state, and he only a junior, but colleges scared of him."

Rob decided to meet Naheem, and to his surprise, things never changed and Naheem came up.

Travis went to VA Tech. It wasn't a surprise when Rob received the tickets to Tech vs. Miami from Travis, the first game he would start.

Rob arrived in Blacksburg and met with Reignah. At first sight, he thought she was beautiful, sexy, but young. She was only twenty, but she had graduated high school before she was seventeen and received her degree from VA Tech right after her twentieth birthday. She had several job offers, but Columbia had a lot to offer, and she ended up settling there.

Rob's thoughts were disturbed by Reignah's entrance. She was wearing a dark purple dress that she filled out perfectly. She came over and poured two shots of Patrón, and they both took a shot. Rob poured two more. She smiled, they toasted, and the two shots disappeared.

Rob lit another Dutch and stood looking at Reignah. She looked so shy, innocent, and she was really quiet, unless she got to know you. That, along with the sad, but sexy eyes, pulled Rob to her. Any guy would be crazy not to try and pull up on her.

Reignah eased up to Rob and hugged him. She grabbed the remote to the stereo and changed the CD to Keyshia Cole and pressed 12, a song with Eve. She stepped back and started singing with the song

The words melted in his heart and made him weak to her. She made the softness come out in him.

She stared back at him, the Patrón making her eyes tighter than usual. She meant every word. She loved this big-ass nigga, and he was all hers. If she loved hard, he loved hard, if she acted up and tripped out, he loved harder. She finally realized he was hers. The thought of another man touching her was some bull-shit, as was the thought of bitches touching him or him touching them.

"How many bitches you been with?" she asked out of nowhere, far from the track he was on.

"I don't know. How many niggas you done fucked, or gave head, fucking with them white boys at Tech?" Rob really didn't want her to answer that question, but she was always straightforward, always answering anything he asked.

"Six, and I gave three head, including you. Four were relationships, one was a white boy that I thought I liked, and the other was a friend who hung around all the time. One night drinking, I wanted some, and we did it. Only once. Shouldn't have ever happen . . . fucked up a good friendship," she said. "And you?"

"Maybe ten," he said, ashamed to tell the truth. Counting girlfriends, friends, one-nighters, and tricking, Rob had been in at least fifty bitches.

"You lying. I thought you were a player." Reignah laughed.

"Not me, baby," he said, pulling her to him. "Not me, baby girl."

Chapter Nine

Wednesday, July 20, 2005

I had just jumped out the shower. I was already running late for my meeting. Me and my cousin Rob had started a landscaping service. The work wasn't shit, but getting the big contracts was. My phone was steady ringing.

"What up, private?" I said to the young boy I had holding down an entire street in a section of Virginia Beach called Briarwood Apartments.

Now I had these four ex-Navy guys that hustled on what I call my street. Actually they lived in the apartments, but the money was made in these townhomes called Lake Edward. I knew these cats from balling at the base. They were about getting money, supposed to be street cats from New York, Detroit, and two from Carolina, Raleigh. They got out of the Navy as soon as their time was up, but while living in Briarwood, they realized they could make a spot and get money, so with my backing, they moved out on West Hastings.

Out of respect, I went out and hollered at niggas,

found out niggas were doing most of their hustling on East Hastings and Red Horse. So I set those boys up, and money was real good. Until they came to me one day with a bullshit sob story.

"Whole bunch of those dudes moved in on us. I said something, they came wrong. New York pulled the burner, but they had mad guns. We left."

"Who in charge? Anybody stand out?" I asked. I had already talked with those niggas, and they did this shit before.

"Yeah, two cats. Big-ass dude, thick nigga name Mo. Had two guns. And some nigga Strap, acting like he didn't give a fuck, hollering shit."

"All right, chill. We going back out there about six," I said and hung up. I hit 2 on my speed dial. "Ma," I said as soon as she picked up.

"What's wrong with you, boy?" she asked. "Everything okay?"

"Always good, Ma. Call Sister Johnson and tell her to tell Sidney I really wish I could see him."

"Okay, I'll call you back."

She never called back, but I know she called, and they probably started talking. Far as I knew, it had been six hours and they could still be on the phone.

The day went fast.

I returned home at about seven thirty. The shadow on the sofa was no other than my man. A smile came across his face. We hugged.

"What up, baby?" I yelled.

"I been waiting to kill a man. You late. Now I got to kill you too," Sidney said.

We laughed, but the smiles didn't mean we were playing.

I went to the closet and pulled up my floorboard,

pulled out my black .380. Sidney grabbed my .45, and out the door we went. I called my boys and told them to go to work.

We left the car up by the boulevard and arrived on foot, through the back. Me and Sidney stood back while they worked and watched the cats across the street. Sidney already had his eye on Mo and Strap. I knew the routine. These cats were playing.

A white Expedition pulled up slowly and stopped, and Mo began to walk to the truck.

I turned, and Sidney was in motion, headed for the front of the truck. I was swift and low. The .380 came out, and I ran from behind the truck.

From the look in Mo's eyes, he knew he was gone. I gathered he would have begged, pleaded, and cried if he had a chance.

One shot to his neck and one to his chest, left on West Hastings, his big-ass crumbled body lying cold.

But before the *BANG*! had stopped ringing in your ear, the distinctive .45 went off. Then you heard and seen niggas scattering, leaving the second motionless body. Strap.

The block got hot, and the money stopped for a second, but I was trying to see my way back. I was missing that money like crazy.

I eased my way back on W. Hasting. I didn't drop a lot of shit on them. I couldn't afford the loss if some shit went down.

I even went out there and hooped with my young-'uns, draped in all black with two black .380's.

After I let them go, and later a few rough nights and calmer weeks, money was flowing. As soon as I dropped a brick on them, things were moving that fast.

I was expecting to get seen real quick with my money,

but I didn't get a call at all. I kept trying to reach them and decided I would go by later and see what the fuck was going on.

I was sitting at home when my phone rang. "Hello," I answered.

"Hi, Bigg. Just wanted to call and let you know your son is doing fine," she said.

I got quiet.

"Ree-Ree, I told you—"

"Bigg, I can't express it no other way. He knows you as *daddy*, you know him as your son. Sorry, but I don't know. You know my heart."

"How is he coming along?"

I hated her saying he was my son because he really wasn't. It made me feel funny inside. But I couldn't say shit because I was still fucking her, and she was still serving me better than when I was with her.

I questioned why she would do this to Buck, a nigga that was giving her everything. Many nights after we'd fucked for hours passionately, as if love was still there, she would express that she cared for Buck and respected and loved what he'd done for her, but she was in love with me and dreamed for the day I would say, "Come home."

I heard her words, but I kept convincing myself that she wasn't shit. I would never let bygones be bygones. That stayed in my head, and I just fucked.

"He's better. Seeing you would be all that to him."

I was quiet. I was thinking, *Maybe I should before he goes home to Buck's house.* I definitely wasn't welcome over there.

"I'll try and stop through later. I got to check on my money out The Lakes. Niggas got me fucked up."

I had told Ree-Ree all about shit going on through pillow talk. She was around when I was new to the game and had advised me through stories of her cousins and friends she'd grown up with, an education within itself. She was my road dog, and we kicked it hard. That's why it was so hard fucking with her, trying to smother emotions. She had me so confused, I just wanted to hang up.

"Call me after you finish, Bigg. Please."

"Gotcha, man."

"I love you, Bigg. I got real love, baby!" Ree-Ree hung up.

I sat there shaking my head. I couldn't believe the shit I was going through with this bitch.

I snapped back with a smile when my phone rang. It was my Lake Edward money calling. "What up, son?" I answered.

"What up, Bigg?"

"Where y'all niggas been?"

"Trying to finish up grinding, son," he answered.

"Y'all niggas done?" I asked, trying not to show my excitement.

"Done and waiting. They still out there."

"See you in a few," I said, jumping up.

I went to my cabinet under the sink and pulled out my pots and pans. I lifted up the wooden base, reached to the left under the floor, and pulled out one of the two bricks left.

I threw it in a bag and jumped in the new Tahoe, headed out this bullshit projects called Lake Edward. I turned off Newtown Road. I wanted to see how shit was moving on West Hastings, so I cruised through, but all I saw was a few LE boys hanging out, kids playing, but no money being made.

I got to the apartment and knocked.

"Who that?" a voice said.

"Open the door, fool. It's Bigg."

The door opened, and the New York cat stood in the door.

I walked in, and the door shut. Two cats were standing behind the door. My heart dropped.

I reached for my burner, but the right blow knocked me against the couch, which stunned me, but the chrome .45 stopped me in my tracks.

I was bound with duct tape and dragged into the back room, where I saw the two Carolina niggas tied to two chairs, both naked and their bodies mutilated. They had deep, open gashes. They were severely beaten and drenched with gas, and rags were stuffed in their mouths, duct tape around their mouths and heads. Their eyes were open, and they cried for help, but all you saw was tears. No screams got out.

I stared at the tall brown-skinned kid with dreads. He looked so familiar. He rocked a long beard like mine, and could've easily been mistaken for a Muslim doing good in the street. He looked like a chill guy, but the blood on his hands let me know this was his work.

I couldn't believe this New York nigga got in bed with these niggas. They must have been from "Up Top," folks he'd brought down.

"Where the re-up shit?" New York asked.

"Didn't bring it. Came to pick up money. I ain't got it like that."

"You better, baby boy. I hope you ain't come like that. Crown need that shit, baby." The tall light-skinned nigga was holding the chrome .45. "That nigga ain't hear you, Crown."

"Make that nigga talk, Laudi-Daudi." All four of Crown's front teeth gleamed from the gold crowns.

Laudi pulled a machete from the closet. "Turn him on his stomach!" he yelled. "And tape his mouth."

I was flat on my stomach when I felt the sharp-edged machete going down my spine, cutting me as if I wasn't even wearing a shirt. As he cut, my agony and grunts could only be seen in my eyes.

I looked up at New York and wanted to kill him. I stared deep in his eyes with hatred. Then I saw Crown grab the gas can.

I squirmed and fought, bracing myself as the gasoline hit the open wounds. My body screamed, 'cause I couldn't. I shook. I stared at New York, but it wasn't hatred in my eyes, it was a cry for help. My tears were saying help me, but he did nothing.

They sat me up and snatched the tape off my mouth.

"Where's the shit?" Laudi asked.

"Talk to me, homie. We gotta go." Crown smiled at New York.

My mind went to my military days. "United States Marine, *Semper Fi*. United States Marine, *Semper Fi*," I repeated.

"Nigga think he a prisoner of war or some shit, Laudi," Crown said.

"Naw. That nigga a clown. Get his keys and check his whip," Laudi told New York.

Two minutes later, he came back with the bag.

They stood smiling. They stared at the Carolina boys in the chair, not moving, their heads slumped to their chests.

"See if your ass can swim in the tub face down like the other nigga."

Detroit had put up so much of a fight, they drowned him in the tub with hot-ass water.

My back was stuck to the wall, from all the blood. They gathered the drugs and money and walked in front of me.

Crown pointed the .45 at my head. "Gotta make sure he don't talk, Laudi," he said.

"Gotcha. Do it like this, fuckin' clown! You ain't no soldier, nigga. I'm a soldier, soldier in these streets. You's a military soldier, and I'm telling you, soldier to soldier, stay out these fuckin' streets and out of the Lakes. This shit ain't for you." Then he took the machete, put it across my mouth with the sharp edge in the crease, and sliced my cheek wide open.

The bottom part of my mouth fell, and I fell over from the pain. I lay with my eyes shut as they exited the room.

Seconds later, I heard Laudi yell, "Crown, you didn't put in no work! Put in some work!"

Then I heard two shots. The door opened, and then it closed.

I fell headfirst to the floor still unable to move, unable to speak, or make any noise. I was relieved. I was still alive. Somebody was coming. Somebody.

Chapter Ten

Wednesday, August 17, 2005

This was the first time we'd all come together for about a month.

"Damn, soldiers! We gotta figure out something. I'm outta how much?" Fox looked at Butch.

"Five kilos since y'all man Bink got done up. Two with him and three with your man right here." Butch motioned his head in my direction.

I sat there with my lips pressed together, my jaw sewed and wired. Major nerves had been damaged, and I had no feeling in my face. This dread had given me a "buck fifty" to wear for life.

Everybody sat in silence, looking around at each other, listening to Fox discuss his losses. We all respected him for what he'd introduced us to, but this wasn't part of the game. We saw the potential to make fast money, easy money. All we had to do was play the role, but the murder, robbing, and torture was more than we asked for, at least me and Bink, who was dead after going through the surgeries and rehabilitation.

Fox didn't seem to be himself, and was truly upset about his losses. But what could we do?

"So you gonna be all right, Bigg?" Rob made his way over to me.

I was moving slow, but my body was fine. My face and jaw felt heavy, but I was all right, except for the eighteen-pound weight loss from not eating anything. I had a machine with a tube going into my mouth and through which broth was pumped very slowly onto my tongue so I wouldn't choke.

A month later, I'd be sucking broth. The doctors said I was coming along fast, but I still had no feeling. Physically, I was recovering. Mentally, this shit had me fucked up.

I nodded my head at Rob and gave him a pound, letting him know I was fine.

"Sorry about this shit," Rob said. "For real."

I waved my hand like it was nothing.

"I know Bink dead and we all moving his shit to keep things going, but we short over here," Fox said, looking at me. "How you plan to make this up, Bigg?"

I just stared at him.

"Nigga fucked up, sir!" Rob said.

"Can't you give him some time?" Sidney asked.

"I don't have time. He needs to come off ten grand or something. Pay something on the bill," Fox said loudly.

I patted my hand down, as if to say lower your voice. Things seemed tense.

"Bigg, maybe you need to make some runs and put in some work. You owe me forty-five grand," Fox said.

"You'll get your money, dog!" Rob said. "Calm down. Ain't nobody trying to get you."

"Naw, he got got. He slipped. Not my fault. Should have been prepared for this type shit," Fox yelled.

"And you should be prepared," Sidney said.

"But I didn't get got soldier," Fox said.

I pulled out the pad I'd been writing on and turned it over to Fox.

I'M DONE! I DON'T HAVE NO DOUGH SAVED, AND THEY GOT ME FOR THE THREE BRICKS. ALL THIS DRUG SHIT AIN'T ME. I'M DONE! SORRY ABOUT YOUR LOSS.

"Fuck that! You ain't paying me?"

"Chill, Fox. Don't act up in front of company," Rob said, referring to Butch.

"I ain't company," Butch said. "I'm a soldier under Fox command. What?"

"But you ain't family, and Fox shouldn't of brought you," Rob said. "For real, some things are left to us four, no add-on niggas."

Fox stepped toward Rob. "This is my shit, and I open and close doors. You don't. This is about my money and how I'm going to recap my losses, soldiers."

I held up my paper.

I HAVE NOTTHING. I CAN'T DO SHIT, AND I'M DONE WITH THIS DRUG SHIT. COUNT ME OUT.

"You ain't going nowhere until my money straight. I don't care if you got to sell this house and all the shit in it," Fox said.

Butch laughed, and Fox gave him a pound like they'd grown up together. As the words slid out his mouth and reinforced his new connection to Butch, it was as if the chains were broken.

I blinked, and when my eyes opened, I felt no love for this nigga. A burst of adrenaline rushed my body. My eyes squinted, and I threw my hands in the air, to let him know I didn't give a fuck. Then I pointed to the door.

"We still got business," Fox said.

"Naw, your business is over with. Get the fuck out of here," Sidney said, no expression whatsoever.

Butch shifted his weight to one leg and put his hand on his waist.

Sidney said to Butch, "Don't move again." Then he stared back at Fox.

"Where is this going, Sidney?" Fox asked with a smile. He looked at Butch, who shook his head.

"I said not to move," Sidney said, and in a split second, before we all saw the 9 mm come out, he shot Butch, who fell, the bullet going straight through his side.

"Need you ask again, or were you saying bye?" Sidney stared into Fox's eyes.

With Rob's assistance, Fox grabbed his man, and they walked him out to the car and drove off.

Rob walked back in the house and looked at me and Sidney. He shook his head. "You didn't have to shoot a nigga, soldier."

"Fuck him!" Sidney said. "I'm done with all this shit. If Bigg done, I'm done. And I think he for real. Look at my man. Bigg, pretty nigga, face cut the fuck up."

"So be it," Rob said. "But don't kill a nigga. I still got to get mine. I can't stop right now!"

"Well, you better hurry up and find another connect because dude mouth and actions just ended his king-pin career. I wasn't with all this shit anyway."

"He dude now, acting like Fox hadn't looked out for all of us. Fact be told, you didn't get down, and you made money, and you still getting money, soldier," Rob said.

"Maybe you got it fucked up. Bigg like my brother, y'all niggas my friends. I'll do all y'all niggas to make sure he all right. Those are my last words, soldier."

"Talk to your man, Bigg," Rob said, giving me a pound. "Take it easy, Sidney." Then he walked out the door.

The day had gotten away.

I heard the garage door open. We looked outside to see the CLS pulling in. Ree-Ree had just gotten off work. She had gotten a job at GEICO and was handling hers.

From the time the police had arrived and the ambulance pulled me from the apartment, she was there. She had called Rob, because I wasn't answering my phone. They rode out the Lakes just in time to see me being pulled out on a stretcher. Their first sight was New York being bagged by the coroner. Ree-Ree was hysterical. Rob had to calm her down. She cried like a baby when she saw me, tears of joy from me still being alive and what Laudi had done to my face, leaving me a permanent smile.

She rode to the hospital with me and never left my side. When I went home, she asked if she could use my truck. I was cautious, but she had been there like no other. She'd been gone two hours and fifteen minutes. I know because I missed her every minute she was gone with crazy thoughts that could easily become a reality.

When she pulled up, she had her things and our son. She put her shit in my room, his shit in the other room that was once his.

She came and sat down next to me and looked me in
the eyes. "I love you, Bigg. I'm here for you, Bigg, you
and our son only, forever. Please just let me be here. I
was straight with Buck, and I left," she said, touching
my face.

I stared into her eyes. At that moment, I loved her,
and it hurt me that I had hurt her and that we had gone
through so much shit. But as I looked into her eyes and
she took me in her arms, I knew I loved her and needed
her, but I had to tell her what she was coming into. I
wrote:

*I DON'T HAVE NO REAL DOUGH. I'M NOT HUS-
TLING NO MORE. THE SHIT I GOT, I'M GONNA
NEED HELP HOLDING ON TO. FUCKING WITH ME
AIN'T GONNA BE EASY, SO BE SURE.*

She read it and said, "I'm making money now. I'll
drive the CLS and pay for it. And somehow we will
manage. I love you, I love our family, we gonna be all
right." She smiled and hugged me tight.

I held her. I truly believed her.

She rolled up a Backwoods, lit it, and took a deep
pull. Then she leaned in, placed her lips on mine, and
blew the haze slowly into my mouth. The next couple
of shots were shotguns directly into my nose.

I leaned back and went into deep thought. This shit
with Fox was really bothering me, but I had been
robbed and I had one brick left. Without it, I was ass
out. So it was my way of coming off my loss. It wasn't
a choice, it was something I had to do, but I knew it
would cost me a business partner and possibly a friend.

About this time Sidney came out of the room. "So
what's your next move?" he said. "Know you got a
plan."

I grabbed my pad and began to write.

He pushed the pad away. "Get out of here a minute," he said to Ree-Ree directly.

She looked at me. She knew I was with him. She knew of Sidney and removed herself without a word.

"You been fucked up over a month. Talk to me. What's up next? Fuck how you sound. Remember how pathetic you sounded singing in that church in Southern Pines?" He smiled. " 'Take Me Back' by Andrae Crouch." He laughed.

I tried to laugh, but it really hurt.

"Now talk to me, Bigg," he said, sitting close.

"Call . . . Li'l Nate and move this last . . . brick. And go get . . . a job," I tried to say. What usually took seconds to say was taking thirty.

"What about Fox?"

"Fuck him," I said.

"And last but not least, the soldiers that put in this work," he said, putting his index finger on my cut face.

I looked at him, stared into his eyes. Then I dropped my head.

At that moment without my saying it, Sidney knew I didn't want no parts of Laudi or Crown. I wasn't a killer, but I had killed. I wasn't a gangster, but I'd done gangster shit, but that boy was on some other shit, some shit that changed my ways. Some shit I wasn't built for.

Sidney reached over and hugged me then stood up and walked over to the door. "Yo, you got to get it together. You used to this money, Bigg. It's not gonna be easy to stop. Stop because you wanna stop. Don't get stopped on foreign land by no VA cat. You a soldier, man, and you just got some battle scars. But you survived." He looked back at me.

I looked at him and nodded my head. He was right. I

was stronger than I was feeling, but to have your life in another man's hands was something I never thought would happen to me.

"Yo, let's go for a ride," Sidney said.

I got up and walked to the kitchen to let Ree-Ree know I was going out. It was really my first time going out, except for doctor appointments.

We jumped in the Tahoe, headed to the scene of the crime. As he turned into Lake Edward off Newtown, my stomach began to churn, and as we approached the apartment, it turned into a knot.

I guided him through those drug-infested streets with row houses built in the '70s. Many kids out, but little activity.

"Niggas ain't out, for real." Sidney drove slowly, really taking in the area. "It's a lot of cuts, back streets, alleyways, long-ass alleyways, big-ass lake. This shit was made for a trap."

I just nodded my head in agreement.

As he drove around West Hastings, he came back to Lake Edward Drive. He crossed over, and it was like the world changed. Row houses on the right and left, making you feel closed in. Kid, friends, dirty women walking fast, trying to make money. Dirty niggas in work clothes, scoring after work. And young boys in white tees, jeans, and white DCs, all moving fast, running from the car in the street to the alley, from a car to a parked car, from the house to a car. The streets were on fire.

I saw a group of niggas standing by a silver Magnum. The first thing I noticed was the long dreads and long beard. I slumped in the seat and leaned the chair back.

"Tall dread is Laudi. All black, Crown. Big nigga name Poppa. Don't know the other little niggas."

"Stay low," Sidney said as he took in Laudi, Crown, and Poppa all in a glance. He would know the niggas anywhere now.

It wasn't until we turned back on Lake Edward Drive and headed out that my body relaxed, and my adrenaline slowed down.

Chapter Eleven

Wednesday, September 21, 2005

Rob, with another win under his belt, walked out of the field house headed to his truck. As he walked to the parking lot, he noticed the players and the crowd that had formed outside the gate. Then he saw his two key players, Naheem and his cousin LE. Naheem had four shorties around his 2003 Tahoe sitting on 23's and dripping with a light baby blue candy paint.

When their eyes met, Naheem smiled the biggest smile, showing his fronts, his small diamond studs in both ears glistening. He threw his hand up. "A'ight, coach!" he yelled.

LE looked to see who Naheem was yelling at. He looked at the coach and threw his head up. He knew that Coach Rob had helped Naheem's mom get a new apartment in his district just so Naheem could play football for him.

It didn't take much for LE's mom to use her sister's address and change LE's school. The two sisters had dreamed of their sons playing together and following in Travis' footsteps. LE knew Coach Rob had put his big brother, Travis, on. Then later Naheem had given him the rundown. He knew his cousin was Rob's connect to the streets, and Naheem was getting him plenty of money. What Rob didn't know was that Travis was hustling in Blacksburg, and that him and Naheem was running shit to him on weekends.

LE supported Travis and Naheem, but he didn't sell drugs. He was truly along for the ride. He loved his cousins, but he hated drugs, hustlers, and fake niggas. LE worked four days a week cleaning two banks from six to eleven, and made $1,000 a month. Between football and his job, it left no time for trouble, and he knew, without Coach Rob, his peoples couldn't do what they do on the level they did it.

Coach Rob threw his hand up to Naheem and pointed at LE. He knew his relationship with them both, but through hidden feelings, they depended on Coach Rob to guide them to a college level, which he was doing.

Rob jumped in his truck. As he headed home, his life began to play in his mind. Things weren't the same. Bigg was out the game, Fox was on edge, and dealing with him wasn't the same. Reignah was the only thing in his life that seemed right.

She was wonderful, but lately her being insecure was wearing him down. Every day it was something new, either a different question about his past life, or the things he had going on. And if he changed his routine to satisfy her worries, she would fuss or bring up something that she'd snooped around and found from the past.

He loved her, but he had to keep reminding himself

that she was young and that no matter how smart and focused she was, how hard she worked, and appeared to be a woman, she still hadn't experienced much in life, and had the sensitivity and emotions of a young woman and didn't know totally how to handle certain situations.

He pulled up to his house. Walking in, he didn't realize she was home. He walked into the room, and there she sat in the chair looking at TV.

"How are you? I thought you were 'sleep or gone out."

"Where you been?"

"You know I had a game. Why you asking simple-ass questions?" Rob had gotten used to the bullshit and was already on the defensive when he came in the house.

"It's one in the fuckin' morning. High school games are over by eleven."

"Met with the boys, talked with the other coaches, met them at the pub down the street from the school."

"Oh! You been drinking. You have a good time?"

"Yeah, it was work and business." Rob laughed.

"Glad you think shit funny." Reignah jumped up and slapped the drink out of his hand and then the ashtray that held the Dutch. She stood in front of him.

He grabbed her wrist, squeezed and twisted her skin, making her yell.

"Now pick up the ashtray and the Dutch," he said calmly.

She did it with tears in her eyes.

"Now get a towel and clean that shit up," he said as he held the grip and guided her to the bathroom. As she bent down to clean it up, he let her go.

Tears rolled down her face, as she grabbed her arm,

which was black and blue, and bruised badly. She looked back at him.

He stared into her eyes. "Don't ever go there again," he said calmly. "Control your anger." He grabbed his Dutch and walked to the loft to make another drink.

Reignah threw on her clothes and grabbed some shit.

When he saw her walk down the stairs and out the door, he had Beanie Siegel blasting through the stereo.

Reignah came back in and saw Rob chilling on the couch. She sat down beside him and pulled up her sleeve. "See what you did? You are mean and abusive. I won't stand for it," she said, tears in her eyes.

"You brought that on yourself." He pulled on the Dutch.

Reignah slid off the couch and, before he knew it, slapped him hard cross the left side of his face with a fast right.

He bent down and felt his drink and glass hit him in the head. By the time he jumped up, she was down the stairs and out the door in a hurry. When he got to the door, all he saw was taillights. She had pulled her car out the garage and had it out front running.

He took his T-shirt and wiped his face and head as he walked back upstairs. He grabbed a towel and went to pick the glass up and began to laugh. "That bitch went the fuck off, throwing blows on my ass."

He shook his head and turned everything off, went in his room, undressed and climbed in bed. He leaned back, and at that moment, the loneliness hit him. What was so warm and cozy an hour ago was now so cold. What he was so excited to get home to was now gone.

He turned on his side, gripped the pillow, and fell into a light sleep. At about 7:30, his eyes popped open. The night was long. He was wide-awake. "Awe! I miss you, Reignah." He jumped up, realizing her presence was everything.

He turned on the TV to ESPN and lit the Dutch that had been through hell. The picture of Travis on the screen with the big Virginia Tech logo caught his attention. He turned up the TV, ready for some good news about the all star he coached

"Major drug bust in Blacksburg. A star player for VA Tech was caught with two kilos of cocaine in his truck driving down Highway 64 en route to Newport News. It is said that he has over 25 kilos in the Hampton Roads area. More on this story in a minute."

Without hesitation, jeans on, left boot, right boot, T-shirt, he reached in the closet grabbed his 9 from under the bed, and got the .45. He grabbed the backpack that contained money and four kilos of coke and threw it on his back.

His heart dropped at the *BOOM*! that tore his front door off its hinges. He took a deep breath. *Iraqis didn't fuck with me. Do you think you can?* He ran toward his loft, hitting two officers on the step. His next two steps were across the loft and over the banister. He let off four shots before landing on the plush leather couch. He jumped up as they shot back, hit the floor, and scrambled to the back door and out through the condos in the woods.

Fox had taken Butch to Norfolk General for his gun wound. They gave a report, got him bandaged up, and hit the road. Not much was said on the three and a half hour ride.

"I got to see your man, Captain. This just can't ride," Butch said as they turned off 95.

"You'll never see him again, and if you do, it will be

a sad day for your family. He ain't nobody to fuck with," Fox said, coming to a stop.

Fox was in deep thought, and didn't want to hear that shit Butch was talking. Butch had become his partner and was making money without bringing no problems, but his childhood friends didn't play games. Niggas were in their early twenties, but had seen so much death and so much combat, that life was taken serious early.

"Tell Erica I'll get with y'all tomorrow early. Heah! Keep your head up!" Fox said, pulling off.

Fox's mind went to Bigg. In a split second he had changed everything. Four men thick as thieves. Now two stood together against the others. Even though he wasn't scared of Bigg or Sidney, he just wasn't comfortable being on the outs with them, not to mention, before this, Bigg made money in Tidewater. Real money. He knew the three he dropped on Bigg was money in the bank.

He realized Bigg could have lost his life. He got caught slipping, and somebody made him pay. How the fuck he the only one walk out alive, his whole team dead? "God, thank You for sparing my friend. Thank You," he said out loud.

He reached for his phone and dialed Bigg's number.

"Hello," Ree-Ree said.

"Put Bigg on the phone."

"Hold on." She yelled in the garage, "Fox on the phone."

Bigg came inside and got the phone. "What up?"

"You, I need you to take a second and get yourself together, but I need you to continue moving your share. Take a rest, but I need you. And sorry about not seeing what really could have happened. Talk to you soon."

"All right, sir!" Bigg had no intentions of ever fucking with the game again.

Fox walked in his house. He eased through the dark and hit the light.

Joy stood in a yellow thong and bra, legs spread slightly apart. She hit the switch, and smooth sounds of Maxwell filled the air.

He dropped everything and took off his shirt. All the bullshit that had been running through his mind disappeared, as he focused on the woman in front of him.

She stared him down, taking in his well-defined body. She realized, at that moment, her man was perfect. He handled his business like a disciplined soldier, but he lived the life of a hood cat, creating a swagger any woman could love.

He approached her, and she put both her hands on his chest and slowly brought them down, feeling every muscle in her man's body.

She came down to his pants and undid his belt, and his pants fell around his ankles. She grabbed the bulge that was jumping and trying to get at her. She reached and snatched down the boxer briefs. She slowly and lightly stroked his dick and lowered her warm, wet mouth onto it.

He jumped. She hadn't given him head in almost a year. He stood at attention as her mouth did what he'd thought about for months. A feeling came over his body, and it began to tense. He pushed farther in her mouth to get her off the tip, because he didn't want to let off in her mouth. He'd save that for those hoes in the street. Fucking around on his wife was not his thing, but if a bitch wanted to give him some head, that could be worked out.

He lifted her up and led her to the couch. She laid back and brought her legs back then opened up, and he wasted no time. They hadn't made love in months, and now it was feeling like his first time. Excitement ran through his body as he grabbed his dick and guided into her. She was moist not wet, and snug, not tight, as he entered.

He wanted to slam it home and fuck the shit out of her, but it had been a minute, and she wanted to make love. He knew her. He slowly worked his head in down to the shaft and he slowly guided it in and out, up and down. He looked down, his hand wrapped around his manhood, and liked the vision of his dick extending out of his hand and into his wife. It was like drilling for oil. He did it slowly, until he realized the wetness soaked his fingers.

Joy's breathing had increased, her mouth slightly open, as she spread her legs as far as they could go, trying and wishing he could give her more dick.

As she squeezed her pussy, he felt her walls tighten on his dick, and he removed his hand, allowing himself to fall into heaven.

He sat still for about thirty seconds, enjoying the feeling that took over his entire body. He slowly began to move, but her motions were causing him to lose rhythm. He raised up as if he was doing a push-up and slid in hard, forcing every inch of dick in her, and began to pound, meaning to slow her down, but she came back harder, louder, and stronger.

Fox reached down, grabbed the back of her neck, and pulled her back off the bed. Now his face was staring at hers. He lowered his hips and slammed it home over and over, until she slowed down and threw her legs tightly around his waist, dug her nails into his back, and held her breath.

He held her tight as he shoved his dick deep in her while being still, making his dick jump as she came all over him. She squeezed him as she shook. They stared deep into each other's eyes, and she fell back and collapsed, her arms and legs sprawled out, all her energy gone.

He assumed the push-up position and slowly began going in and out of her. Slowly she started to move as her husband's stiff body rested only inches over hers with only the squishing sounds of him going in and out of her. They looked at each other and smiled. Joy thought they were gonna be all right in time.

Fox had thoughts of fucking the shit out of her in every way. He didn't know when this was coming again.

Joy ran the soaped rag across Fox's back, as he allowed the water to run over his head. He tried to ease his mind. His street shit was running lovely, but his home life was a wreck. And even though he tried to block it out, it was there to deal with.

Now that Joy was coming around and acting like she had some sense, his street shit was falling apart. He came back to reality when he heard her soft voice.

"So what's going on with you?" Joy asked as she exited the shower. She could tell something was pulling his mind somewhere else.

"What you mean?" he asked with attitude, figuring he better hurry up and get out before she started wilding out. He saw the sudden change and thought the crazy woman was back.

"Come here," she said, holding the towel as he stepped out the shower.

She began to dry him off from head to toe then wrapped the towel around him and kissed the left side of his chest, right on his tattooed wings that read *82nd Airborne* above it.

"Now, the other night, I had a dream that was so real. Everybody was against you, and you didn't know where to turn. And I wasn't here for you." She stared into his eyes. "They killed you, and I didn't know what to do. I woke up crying like it was so real. But I started praying like my grandma showed me. I prayed that you'd be okay, and for Him to help me. And it's like I could hear my grandmother saying, 'It ain't nothing but the devil and that evil spirit trying to break you, but put your hand up to God and rebuke that evil spirit. That devil is a lie.' I could hear her so clearly.

"I stood up, threw my hands up, and gave it all to God." Joy threw her hands up demonstrating. "Something came over me, and all I know, I laid down and slept like I haven't in months. When I woke up, I felt rested and strong. I felt like the old Joy, and that's who in front of you now. Now what the hell is going on with you? Talk to me, baby. I got you." Joy inched closer to his face and kissed him then turned and walked out.

Fox stared at her ass as she walked out. She'd surprised him, but that's the girl he fell in love with. God had answered his prayers.

"I hope this new Joy want to fuck like the old Joy did," he said out loud.

"You ain't ready, you ain't ready!" she said from the bedroom.

"Shit!" He grabbed his dick and looked at himself in the mirror.

"Your phone ringing back to back. Something wrong?"

"Naw. Bigg got fucked up and got robbed, so he short. Nobody in Fayetteville. All I got is Columbia, Richmond, and D.C. Fayetteville and Norfolk was my money-makers. I'm coming up short."

"We can live off Columbia and here alone."

"You can live off that shit, I can't."

"You'll learn. You will leave. Now let's get something to eat and answer your phone."

Fox pulled out his BlackBerry from the pouch and saw that he had two missed calls, both from Bigg, and dialed it back.

Chapter Twelve

"Yeah. What's going on?" Fox asked.

"They kicked Rob crib in. He gone."

"Feds?" a shocked Fox asked.

"Naw, state police. He got away but killed one officer and wounded two more then escaped into the woods." I was upset they came for my boy, but glad he trooped. "Eighty-second Airborne Paratrooper til we die."

"Til we die, soldier, til we die."

"His girl cousin called. She go to school at VA Tech. She said the young'un talking, but all he know is Coach Rob at his high school. That's how they got him. Tell him to call me on Ree-Ree phone," I said, sliding the responsibility on him to go see Rob.

"Shit! You gonna let me know, soldier, and you gonna find out soon . . . the whole story. Then report to me, face to face. I need you to do shit, Bigg. All this shit falling apart," he said in a worried tone.

"All right, sir," I said, giving him his respect.

Fox had tried to look out for all of us, and we made

him a lot of money. But now it was all falling apart, and not because of him. We already had a place strictly for if this shit happened and somebody was on the run. So it was up to me to go see exactly what went down with Rob and who knew what.

I walked into the bedroom, where Ree-Ree was lying in bed reading a book called *Black Reign*. "Fuck you reading now?" I said.

"Hold tight. Gimme a sec," she said, holding up her hand.

"Put that shit down. I got to go out of town for a sec and see what's up with Rob."

"You disturb me with that. I'm reading the best book I ever read in my life and you come with that shit. All right, Bigg. Where you going? Who going with you? How long you gonna be gone? And what the fuck you going to do, because your ass don't hustle no more. Got another bitch you going to meet? Or is it all a secret and you can't tell me?"

"I'm not even gonna entertain that shit you talking, bitch."

"You must've lost your goddamn mind, nigga!" Ree-Ree dropped her book, and standing on her feet, got into a boxing stance.

I looked at her in her wife-beater and thong, her nipples sticking out and showing clear through the T-shirt. Before she knew it, I grabbed her arm and snatched her, scooped her up, and slammed her on the bed. As her legs flew open, I grabbed the left and pulled her to me.

"You must've lost your mind, jumping up at me. You are my bitch, and I'm gonna give my bitch her dick," I said, forcing myself to talk.

It hurt like hell, and I drooled with every word, but

fuck it, I had to get back. Look what this pussy was doing.

As I reached in my sweats and exposed myself, I fell on top of her and reached down and pulled the thong to the side and guided myself in her. She gasped as I forced myself inside and began to pound. I grabbed the back of her head and gripped her hair, staring in her widened eyes.

"No, Bigg. No! Stop! Stop, Bigg!"

"Naw! You suppose to be the baddest bitch! Give it here." I kept pounding as I dominated her body without her consent, and my manhood began to swell inside of her even more. "Whose is it?" I tried to slam my balls in her. "Whose is it?"

"It ain't yours, nigga," she said, looking me dead in my eyes with a blank expression. "Bitch nigga can't handle this pussy." She opened her legs wider. She had scooted her ass to the edge of the bed and had her legs bent but spread wide. "This pussy beating yo' ass. Look at you starting to sweat!"

I began to pound faster and harder. I began to hear her gasp between words. I was breaking her. That's when I slowed down, leaned over, and took a tittie in my mouth. Then I took my other hand and squeezed her left nipple between my fingers as I slow-dicked her ass.

She began to buck on my dick, trying to get it all. "Don't stop, Bigg, don't stop. Please, baby, baby, baby," she screamed, gripping my ass and pulling me deep in her. She wouldn't let me move as she shook and shook then collapsed.

I immediately lifted her up and removed her thong, slid her back on the bed, and put my arms behind her knees and opened her up. I slid my dick back in, and moments later, the feeling that starts in your groin and shoots up to your head and down to your feet and takes control of your entire body for about five seconds came. I dropped her legs and collapsed on top of her as my body twitched.

"You got the best pussy, baby! But I still got to go check my man when I wake up."

Ree-Ree slid up on the pillow and opened her arms, and I fell into them and rested my head on her chest then squeezed her. I was more than happy to have her there.

I was trying my hardest to rebuild my trust in her, but the question remained, Was I starting to feel her again? Was it the fact she was sexy, beautiful, and the sex was crazy, or did I feel I owed her because she was there to nurse me back, hold me down and give all of herself and time to me? She cooked, put straws in juice, warmed up my broth, and fed me teaspoon by teaspoon. She put Neosporin on my bruises, took care of me like her child, and that she didn't have to do. Buck was giving her everything I had to give her and more.

The thought brought tears to my eyes, and I widened them before she saw a tear fall. But I couldn't stop it, so I yawned real hard, covered my mouth, and wiped my eyes then lay back in her arms.

"So what you going to do, Bigg?"

"What you mean?"

"You say you out the game, but you still fuckin' with your peoples."

"Naw. I'm just going to check and make sure Rob all right."

"Then what?"

"Gotdamn! What's with all the questions?"

"Because I'm here with you, nigga. We are a family now, and what you do concerns me, you, and our son. Say what you want, you can't raise a boy like your son and give him unconditional love then cut off all feelings. I know you have mixed feelings about a lot of this shit, but I'm here now, you here now, and we're going forward." Ree-Ree sat up.

"Okay, we here now. So what do this relationship got to do with my muthafuckin' business?"

"If you find a job and go work, NOTHING. But if you gonna play these streets, then a whole lot."

I shook my head. *This simple-ass girl.* "What the fuck do you think you can tell me, girl?" I stood up and wiped my mouth. I was talking more, but I was drooling up a storm. I wasn't ashamed in front of Ree-Ree, but it hurt like hell and she could tell.

"If you listen, I can tell you how to stay alive, how not to get fucked up, how to stay on the street, and how not to get another buck fifty on the other side of your face." She stood up and pointed in my face.

I thought she went too far and was taking me for soft. I wanted to slap her ass.

"Look, Bigg, you do reckless things, and you worry about shit that you shouldn't give a second thought. If the man haven't kicked in our house, it's a matter of time. We need to move. Rob is hot as hell. You need to stay away from him. You owe Fox and you worried. You doing shit because you feel bad because you lost some product. This is the drug game. Y'all shit is business. He making money off you, Rob, the nigga who was with him, and Bink when he was living. Now you going to fuck with him and find him. You need to change your number, move, and do what you gonna do."

"Then what connect I got? What team I got to get money with?"

"Do you want to get back in the game or not? Before I continue, I want you to know I got your back either way."

"I don't know nothing else. I was a grunt in the military, and I'm not going security. It is what it is."

"My closest cousin is doing twenty-five years. This was my brother. I was closer to him than my brothers. When he was home, I was straight. I ran with him and I ran for him. My family was so upset I fucked with him, my dad put me out. It wasn't a thing. My cousin took me in, and I lived with him in a big-ass house in Chesapeake. People thought I was his girl. Anyway, Tru never trusted a soul. When I say never trusted a soul, not his brothers, sisters, momma, cousins, nobody. And the only reason he trusted me . . ." Ree-Ree got quiet and went into a deep stare.

"What?"

"Don't matter what he did. Don't matter. But he came off. Got some money, found a connect, and started his business. He was real nice with his shit, and nobody ever fucked with him, niggas or the police. I watched him hustle for ten years, from fourteen to twenty-four, and never catch a charge. They got him on tax evasion, tax evasion. They knew he sold dope, but could never prove it. I know this shit. I could guide you, but will you listen and let me?"

I heard her and didn't want to admit that she was real convincing. What did I have to lose? I was ass out. "I hear you, and I'm listening."

"You need to find a new connect. Fuck Fox and what you owe him. He ain't gonna do shit. Then get some come-up money, because a new connect ain't fronting you shit."

"Well, my money is real funny."

"You a soldier. Go do the same thing to the next nigga that dude did to you," she said, getting a towel and washcloth. "It's the game, Bigg."

"What? Who the fuck I'm gonna get? And you know that shit ain't me. " I thought she was crazy.

"You gonna get your man Fox, fuck him, rob him for his product and money then kill him." She said it like it was nothing.

"I can't do that."

"Sidney can!" She walked in the bathroom.

Days later I pulled up to the bright yellow raggedy apartment building in Miami Beach. Mad Spanish-talking niggas hanging out. I ran up to the second floor and banged on the door of my man Rock, Spanish nigga originally from New York, but raised on Fort Bragg. His mom married a paratrooper, but his dad was 101st Airborne Division. They lived on the other side of the base in Anzio Acres, but we'd met at Parris Island and instantly became tight, ended up in the same battalion. Then both of us ended up at Camp Geiger near Camp Lejeune.

Once we were both classified as 0311, straight GRUNTs, we did our entire tour together. First Japan, then Cuba, Iraq, and this last tour to Afghanistan broke us both, him along with thousands of other soldiers who just wanted to get back on American soil. That shit was so frustrating, being over there and not knowing why. But this was what we signed up for.

When I went in, I swore to be the best soldier I could

and excel to the highest rank possible by doing my duty and protecting my country, but many of these cats signed up for a job, or to go to school and use the GI Bill, get training while getting a check. But they were away from their family and friends sitting out in the desert, fucking with these people who had no respect for human life. Who would kill themselves in the name of Allah? Many soldiers cracked, committed suicide, came home with illnesses that couldn't be detected, so they go untreated.

The door opened and brought me back.

"What's up, muthafucka?" he said, holding out his hand.

"Same shit," I responded as our hands gripped tightly. None of that hugging shit you see those cats do in the hood.

"So what brings you to Miami?" he asked, as if he didn't know.

"Here to see who you can plug me in with," I said, catching him off guard.

"Fuck you, Bigg! I ain't getting in the middle of y'all shit."

I laughed. "What shit?"

"You, Rob, and Fox shit. I talked to Rob. I know y'all differences. Rob on the run. He on fire and want to come here. Fox don't want to give you shit because you give it away."

"Fuck that! I didn't give shit away."

"Yes, you did, Bigg." He stared at me. "How the fuck you allow yourself to get fucked up? How you allow another nigga to put your life in his hand? We've been through training nobody in the world can fuck with. That shit should not have happened, and you owe that man."

"That's between—"

"Naw, I'm telling you. YOU FUCKED UP! Look at your damn face. We been all over the world fighting, protecting, KILLING," he said slowly and went into a deep stare. "And you let some hood-ass gangsters get you? Just pay that man and apologize."

Rock's phone rang. "What?" he said. "A'ight," he said and headed for the door. "Come on, we gonna shock the shit out of these niggas."

"Who dat, Rock?"

"Rob, Beast, and Cliff."

"Beast down here? I ain't know he was here. Tank from here."

"Beast is from Opalocka, and Cliff from Little Haiti. Those niggas wild. I mean, whoa!" Rock shook his head.

As we came out the building and made our way to the curve, we saw this bright green '77 "deuce and a quarter" sitting high up on some 24's, with sounds banging like you wouldn't believe.

Rob jumped out and threw out his hand, and we gripped tightly. Then he snatched me to him and hugged me like hood cats do. My dude was glad to see me. He was okay, but I really saw that I gave him some comfort.

Cliff jumped out the car with a Heineken in his hand. "Fuck is you doing here, man?" he said, giving me a pound. "Good to see you, Bigg, and you looking well. The war wound healed well," he said, referring to my scar.

I rubbed my scar with my hand.

"Many cats carry that same mark. You learn, and you protect the other side. A'ight." Cliff gave me another pound.

"Bitch, what the fuck you doing in the county of Dade?" Beast yelled from the driver seat. He took a big swig from the bottle of gin.

"Nigga, I go wherever the fuck I please. No bitch nigga better test me." I stared at him.

He took another swig. "Who the fuck you talking to, nigga?" he asked, getting out the car.

This fool had on knickerbockers with black Chucks and long socks. It had to be 110 at the least. It looked like he'd gotten bigger and more defined, and gold covered his entire mouth, top and bottom. He was bald and had a big beard.

"Nigga don't wear shirts in Miami?" I asked this Hulk-looking character coming at me.

"They don't make shirts in my size." He caught my neck with his left hand.

I grabbed his wrist and twisted his arm until his body went down. The right across his jaw would have dropped most men, but I felt a jolt in my groin as my body went in the air, flipped over, and slammed to the ground. I came to my feet, rushed him, and slammed him on his back.

We scuffled for about three minutes before Cliff and Rob stopped us. This wasn't the first time me and Beast locked up, but it was the first time I was happy they stopped it. My body was so sore and my face hurt, but as a Marine and I could overcome anything.

"Still can't fuck with it, Bigg," Beast said.

"Man, I been recuperating from death, and you still couldn't do shit. Gay-ass eighty-second niggas!"

"You want some more of this." Beast hit the wings tattooed on his chest. Then he turned around, and across the top of his back he had *PARATROOPER* and

then below it, *82nd.* "Eighty-second Airborne Paratrooper, my nigga, til I die."

We both stood staring at each other with dirt and
scuff marks all over. He walked over and got his bottle
and took a swig.

"I got to shower, go get some real liquor—Patrón,
Henny, something," I said to Rob. "And some trees.
Beast got you."

"Rock got weed. See him, but I'll run to the liquor
store. I'm almost dry too."

"Bigg," Rob said, "I got away with some cash and
two bricks. Cash is gone, still got two bricks."

I handed him the wad from my right pocket, which
must have been about $800, and he smiled and jumped
in the car with Beast. I hit my left pocket just to make
sure my fifty stacks were still there.

By the time I showered and came out, liquor was
being poured, and weed was in the air. After we all
kicked it for a while, me and Rob made our way back
outside.

"So what you gonna do?" I asked.

"Sell these two ki's, find another connect, and keep
going. I'm on the run now, Bigg. My choices are lim-
ited."

"Got fake ID?"

"Yeah! You know I'm somebody new, but I ain't trying to test it." He smiled.

"So why you haven't moved it?" I asked. "I know
they know somebody."

"I trust these cats to hold me down if we out of state
handling business, but around here, these are their
people, and they might take it all or try, because this is
all I got."

"I feel you. So we out tomorrow. Run to Fayettenam, off two bricks, then come back to Miami and find us a new connect."

"That's what it is, Bigg?" Rob smiled. "I thought you were done?"

"Y'all niggas keep pulling me back in. I can't stop right now."

"In the morning, we grab those two bricks and we out," he said.

Three a.m. came quickly. And we were on the road headed out of Miami Beach. "How long it take, Rob, headed up ninety-five North?"

"Usually it would take twelve hours, but we going to seventy-five. I'm not playing on ninety-five, coming out of Miami in a rental car with two bricks in the cut. We going seventy-five to Atlanta. Make some calls and see what we can do. Remember Carlos?"

"Sanchez. Carlos Sanchez, the Mexican?"

"Yeah. He up there. Let's see what he doing."

We rode up 75 to Atlanta, and Carlos did nothing. He needed us to put him on, but this had to be a fast "up." We needed dough.

We checked out of the Best Western in Marietta and hit the road, 85S to 20E to 95N and hit Fort Bragg/Fayetteville.

I could tell Rob was scared as we came into South Carolina and held his breath til *North Carolina Welcome Us.* "Breathe, nigga, breathe," I said.

We began to make calls and stops. After not being able to move two bricks in one lick, we broke it down, ounce here, four ounces there, quarter ki down there, until we sat in the hotel by the mall counting dough.

"Fifty-four thousand, Bigg! Fifty-four thousand! Thanks, man. This could not have been done without you." Rob handed me ten thousand.

"This could not have been done without me. I ain't saying you owe me half, but act like you know me, nigga," I said, staring in Rob face.

He slid another ten thousand to my side of the table. I stuck out my hand, and we gripped tightly. We gathered our shit and hit 95S back to Miami Beach.

We spent the next week looking for our connect. Many in Miami said they could do it, but we were looking for price and quality.

We finally met somebody through Cliff, this little Haitian dude from around his way. We got a kilo of cocaine for $17,500 and it held a cut to bring back an extra nine ounces.

We made another run to Fayettenam and came back with $33,000 and talked Wyi-Z into giving us two for $33,000. When we arrived back in Miami, we brought back $66,000.

Chapter Thirteen

I had befriended this white girl who was in the Army. She was from Gary, Indiana and fucked with niggas like that. So I started kicking with her, and she became a driver for me and Rob. She even got a spot in her name out in Miami Gardens. She was into fucking me and enjoying herself, but she was all about the money first and then an opportunity to have a place to live in Miami.

We rented a three-bedroom, two-bath, ranch-style house with another apartment in the back behind the garage. Carol Anne lived in the back when she made trips or came on vacation. It was hers. Rob lived in the house. Now he was settled. She drove for him when he had to run to Fayetteville, because I'd made my moves back to VA and Elizabeth City.

My cousins, Rob and Cat, were doing their thing, holding me down, staying closer to me as I built my shit back with the help of Ree-Ree. She was connected to big cats, older cats who needed weight, straight coke, and had cash, so things picked up. I started back strong, making sure this time I stayed on point, like a true soldier, and was waiting for the opportunity to get the big lick.

Me and Ree-Ree got settled, purchased a four-bedroom, two-and-a-half-bathroom, double-garage, 3200-sq.-ft. home out in the Churchland area of Portsmouth, almost Suffolk.

Then she told me we had to make up a baby room. My smile became spaced out, and she asked what was wrong—I was supposed to be happy. But she already knew. She knew there was nothing she could say or do. Just let the nine months play itself out.

I wanted to call my mom and tell her.

I wanted to be happy, to laugh and joke, rub her stomach, and do all the things I did before, but something inside didn't allow me, because I was scared of being a fool again. She used to try to coax me, saying who he or she would look like, but I just smiled. She would hug me and let me know she loved me, wanted me, and desired no one else, but things were hard and didn't seem to be getting any better.

One day I was over at the old house when a car pulled up. The young lady that got out was stunning. She walked up and introduced herself as Reignah.

"Rob girl?" I asked, surprised.

"I was his lady, or that's what I thought," she said in a disappointed tone.

"How is Rob? Haven't seen or heard from him in a minute?" I looked around to see if I saw anyone. I knew she hadn't talked to or seen him, but we had talked. He couldn't contact her anymore, and that was killing him.

"I came across your address in one of his briefcases.

I was praying you knew where he was or even heard from him, Bigg. I'm miserable, I'm lonely. That was my man; he is my life. I can't work, I can't sleep, I can't eat. Sometimes I wish . . ." She fell into my arms, as she tried to stop the tears from rolling down her face.

I held her for a second.

"Sorry. I'm sorry," she said.

"Come in for a minute and get yourself together."

"You still in South Carolina?" she said in a whisper.

"Why you whisper?"

"Just don't know who listening, and I want him to find me. I come home every day praying he'd come find me." She began crying again.

I was impressed. She was thinking like me. I was thinking she might be wired, or somebody was listening. My vibe, though, told me she was sincere, and the way Rob acted, he was missing her too. He was back on his feet and wasn't talking to no bitches, fucking nothing. He just made money and sat quietly at the computer week after week.

I picked up a piece of paper and wrote—DO YOU HAVE MONEY?

"Yes!" she responded.

GO TO THE AIRPORT AND GET A TICKET TO MIAMI. GET A CAB TO SOUTH BEACH AND GO TO A SPOT CALLED WET WILLIES.

We sat down at the computer and looked at flights on cheaptickets.com, flying out of Norfolk International. The flight leaving at six could have her in Miami in a couple of hours. She looked at me strange.

"Go now. Park your shit at the airport and catch that flight," I whispered in her ear. I prayed I wasn't making a mistake.

She squeezed my neck, and out the door she went.

I went inside and retrieved my business phone and called Rob. I found it funny that he was in Edison Court, seeing that was in Little Haiti, where our connect rested.

"So what's going on?" I asked.

"Trying to keep things smooth," he answered, not giving me too much information.

"You resting in Little Haiti?"

"Nah, nah! Met a li'l Haitian thing. Her peoples still in Haiti, but they connected. I'm already in, trying to see if we can get better," he said.

"Be careful, man. They probably all together and connected in some way. Don't get missing," I said seriously, knowing you don't play games with foreigners against their own on their own land.

"Got this, Bigg. I ain't got shit to lose out here, Bigg, so I'm going all out for this money. I'll bury these little dirty muthafuckas without blinking. Just like in Afghanistan, Bigg. Remember?" Rob said, waking me up in more ways than one.

"I remember. And enough said. Now, your girl came by. She found me."

"And," Rob said with excitement and curiosity.

"I told her to go to Wet Willies on the second floor and sit at the bar. She will be there eleven forty-five. It's on you."

"I got to, Bigg. She completes me."

"I know, man. The lady in a nigga life has no idea the true role she play."

"Damn right! The right bitch bring a peace of mind and allow a nigga to really flow. I need her. Thanks, Bigg," Rob said and hung up.

I knew he would be overjoyed at the thought of seeing her. I called his phone back, and there was no answer. I called again, and he picked up.

"What up, Bigg?"

"You hung up too fast. What you gonna do?"

"Shit! I'm gonna go meet her," Rob answered as if I was dumb.

"Suppose the feds on her. Suppose she working with them to save her cousin. I sent her there, but you ain't got to meet her. Man, watch yourself, Rob."

"Damn, man! She ain't that dirty, Bigg," Rob said as if I frustrated him.

"You willing to take that chance?" I asked, really concerned. "It's your freedom we talking about."

"Yeah, she's worth the chance. But I'm on it, I'm not going in blind. I got it. I'll call you later."

Chapter Fourteen

Rob's mind raced a mile a minute. He made it to his Dodge Charger and jumped in, sat still and caught his bearings. *I'll get Carol Anne to come get her and bring her to the house.* At 11:30 he parked the tinted-out Charger on Collins. Carol Anne got out and walked to the strip and strolled down five blocks to Wet Willies. She talked to Rob as she made her way upstairs.

"She should be sitting at the bar."

"It's several people at the bar."

"She's the cutest thing in there," he said proudly.

Carol Anne walked up to the young lady in jeans and a T-shirt and her colorful Air Max. She figured it was Reignah. "Hello. What you drinking?"

"Sex on the Beach. New shit for Miami."

"Not from here?" Carol Anne scoped her surroundings.

"No, but I'm used to the water."

"Carol," Carol Anne said, holding out her hand.

"Reignah," she said, shaking her hand. "Nice to meet you."

"I'm a friend of Rob's. Let's go like we old friends."

Reignah eased off the chair, and they headed out. Carol Anne scoped the area and assured Rob things looked secure. When they made it to the Charger, they entered quickly.

Rob took off even more quickly. He wanted to get the hell out of South Beach. If the peoples came, he would have to shoot it out, but he'd rather that go down in Miami, not South Beach. He dipped off Collins, onto Biscayne, and onto the bridge that led them to Miami. Once he guided onto 95N, he glanced around him, paying extra attention to his rearview. Then he punched it.

He reached out for her hand and took a quick glance at her.

She allowed him to rest his hand in both of hers, and she caressed it. Two tears rolled down her cheeks. She squeezed his hand as tight as she could.

Rob began to soften, and his eyes watered. He quickly cleared his eyes and mind and made his way to his new home in Miami.

After he pulled into the garage and parked, he turned to Reignah and said, "Reignah, this is Carol Anne. Carol Anne, this is Reignah, the love of my life."

"Nice to meet you," Reignah said. *Who is this white bitch?*

"Same here, but it seem like I know you. I've heard a lot about you, but I'm gonna get ready and leave y'all," Carol Anne said, getting out the car. "Because that muthafucka miss yo' ass, for real, girl." She headed through the door to the house and exited out the back to her apartment.

Rob took Reignah's hand and led her inside, through the kitchen, and into the oversized living room.

"Okay, this is nice. From the outside, I thought it was some bullshit."

Rob stared at her, still holding her hand. "Yo' mouth ain't changed. Good to see. I always like that. You never hold nothing back."

"Bright pastel green—You know this old shit is banging."

"This old shit cost two hundred seventy-five grand. What?" Rob said.

"And?"

"And what? Shit ain't cheap down here."

Reignah looked into his eyes. "Well, we need to see five hundred thousand if we staying down here."

Rob smiled. "I've missed you like you wouldn't believe," he said seriously.

"I'm here. I've been going crazy, wondering if you was okay, wondering if my peoples was gonna be okay. I didn't know how to get in touch with nobody you know, but I remember when we stayed in Virginia Beach that time and you went by Bigg house. I loved his house and remembered the street and found him. You know my love. Why you haven't came to find me? You could have, or you happy down here fuckin' that white bitch?"

"Calm your ass down, and let's talk. Sit down and start from that night. Stop at your cousin situation right now."

Rob grabbed two glasses and the Patrón. He sat down on the corner of the loveseat as she sat on the couch right on the side where the couches came together, so they were close and facing each other. He wanted to take in her every word. He poured shots and began rolling a Dutch for the "Kush" he so desperately needed for his racing heart.

"Well, they stopped me when I left the house and got down the street. So I was in the back of the car when they entered the house. I was so scared, because they kept saying, 'armed and dangerous . . . don't take no chances.' I thought you were gonna come out in a bag. I heard all that gunfire and windows crashing, and I prayed like never before. When things started going crazy outside, I was really scared. Then the detective came and told me it was in my best interest to tell them where you would run to. That's when I knew you got away." Reignah smiled, shaking her head as if to say, "Boy, you got me there. How?"

Rob just smiled and let her continue.

"They was on me for hours, til the morning, and then they hit me with conspiracy and some more shit. Held me on fifty thousand. My parents made my bail. They seized the house and everything in it. I'm an accountant, so those charges and my job didn't go together. They let me know it would look better if I resigned. So with no money or job, I went back home. Couple days passed, and my cousin LE came to see me. Travis started talking his ass off, told the police everything. That's why they came after you. He told on Naheem too. Naheem broke out, and ain't nobody heard from him. But, for real, I think he hollered at LE lawyer, told him he gonna get some time, but your capture and connection could lessen his time."

Rob just stared at her. "So you rolling with blood?"

"I'm here, Rob. I left home and didn't tell nobody nothing. I'm with you, baby. By your side forever." She slid closer to him, staring into his eyes as he lit his Dutch.

"Don't get me wrong. I love my cousins, and we like brothers and sisters. Our father raised us real close. I don't want to see them locked, and I don't want to see the man that I can't breathe without away from me. I love you and can't be without you. What are we gonna do?" she added sadly.

"I'm on the run, Reignah. For me, there's only one thing—Stay on the streets and take no chances." He thought about how bad he wanted to snap Travis' neck. "So you here, and if you stay, you running too. Now that's a serious choice. Running with me is not what I want for you. I love you too much. But if you want to stay, really want to stay, your love overpowers my good judgment, and I can't say no. You understand that?"

"Yes, and I'm not leaving your side." She leaned over and kissed him, grabbed the Dutch, and leaned back. "Now, two questions. What's the plan?" she asked seriously. "What you doing in Miami? And who are you?"

"Get Travis out, find Naheem, and come together on some shit. Me and Bigg got our own shit going. Our connect is here in Miami, and Carol Anne help us transport shit to South Carolina and VA. And fuck you mean, who am I?"

"That shit you pulled at the house. The police, news, and everybody was talking about your escape and assaults. It came out that you're military trained. I know military dudes, and they can't do all that."

"Well, I'm trained for war. I have a black belt in karate, and I'm a second degree black belt in tae kwon do. I studied while stationed in Japan. Plus, I'm an eighty-second Airborne Paratrooper." He stood up and snatched off his shirt, turning so she could read the same tattoo on his back she had seen forever. "Do you know what all that mean?"

"What it mean?"

"You fuckin' with a bad muthafucka."

"Got that shit right," she said, knowing this nigga was the truth.

Rob took her hand and guided her to his bedroom. It didn't contain a lot, just the one tall dresser and a full bed. She removed her shirt and jeans, and he took her into his arms and squeezed her. He then laid her on the bed, laid beside her, took her in his arms, as she wrapped her arms around him.

Reignah, her body now relaxed, felt secure again. Her mind wasn't racing, and at this moment, emotionally she was happy and satisfied. She wanted him to get inside of her, but holding him felt so good, she didn't want to let go.

It was if Rob had read her mind, because he never removed his jeans. He just lay there and held her as if she might try and get away. Rob allowed his mind to slowly relax, and his body followed. He hadn't had this feeling since the night the PEOPLES came to get him.

His life had changed drastically overnight, but tonight he felt complete. He felt God had blessed him, and he fell asleep with Reignah wrapped tight in his arms. He fantasized that all the hell they'd gone through was just a bad dream, but every time he opened his eyes, he would take a deep breath and pull her closer.

Chapter Fifteen

I walked into Leigh Memorial. Ree-Ree had just gone into labor. I didn't call nobody, but my mom, because this wasn't something I shared. I cared for her, I felt I even loved her, but in the pit of my stomach, something didn't let me give my all. She felt it at times when we lay together. I would just climb behind her and relieve myself to satisfaction. Yeah, she was still sexy and beautiful, but I knew once she had the baby and I got a blood test, I would be different person.

As I made my way into the room, her sister and cousin stared at me.

"Where the fuck you was?" her cousin Shamar yelled. "This shit already popping and you just walking up in this muthafucka."

"You have to be quiet and carry that outside," the nurse said.

I looked at Shamar gritting at her dike-looking ass, dressed like a nigga. "That's your cue. Now get the fuck

outta here, bitch, and sit your ass down out there." I
eased past her to Ree-Ree.

"Bitch nigga, you must've lost your mind. I don't
give a fuck who you is! I'll lay your punk ass down!"
she yelled.

I looked at her and started to pull my .45 that rested
on my side between my Antik jeans and my wife-
beater. After what I'd been through, I didn't play that
threatening shit. "You best leave, because I will forget
that you are a nasty bitch and slap the man out you!"

"Please, stop!" Ree-Ree said.

They were just getting ready to tell her to push when
I came in. Her words softened me, and I turned to her
and took her hand from her sister. Her sister lived in
Jersey, but they were very close.

Ree-Ree's dad was from the Dominican Republic. He
had come over to the U.S. and had established a lucra-
tive drug business, moving cocaine in New York, D.C.,
Richmond, and Philly. He had fathered nine kids by
seven women, was later caught and deported back to
the Dominican Republic. He later contacted all his
kids and let them know of the others. She had sisters
and brothers up and down the East Coast. She had met
six, four girls and two boys. The other two boys were
locked up, trying to follow their father's shadow.

She had met Torres, NaVante's brother by the same
mother, and they lived in the same beautiful home in
New Jersey. For some reason, Ree-Ree and NaVante got
close, and she loved trips to Jersey and chilling with
him. Their dad had left each woman with enough
money for them to live comfortably even in his ab-
sence. Several woman fucked up their money, but Torres' and NaVante's moms, a Dominican, had married
another Dominican, who was also involved in the dis-

tribution business and was high-ranking in a profitable organization.

I stared down at Ree-Ree as she stared into my eyes. She had a look on her face that I'd never seen before. "It's gonna be okay." I leaned down and kissed her dry lips and ran my hand through her thick, dark hair. "I love you, Ree-Ree. I really love you."

At that moment, all my negative thoughts vanished. I held her hand while NaVante stood close.

NaVante looked at Ree-Ree then down between her legs. "Come on, Ree-Ree. Bring my nephew in here."

"You see it, Navy," Ree-Ree yelled, calling her sister by her nickname. "What you see?"

"Nothing yet."

"Ready. Okay, push," the nurse said. "Wait, wait! Don't push, don't push! Go get Doctor Wells," she said to the other nurse. "Call for him now."

The other nurse ran out the door.

"What's wrong?" I asked the nurse. "What is wrong?" I said again as the nurse stared down at Ree-Ree.

Doctor Wells came rushing in. He looked down between Ree-Ree's legs and told the nurse to get some forceps and that he needed two more nurses.

"*¿Qué estás haciendo?*" NaVante asked the nurse in Spanish.

The nurse answered her in Spanish.

"*¡Dios mio!*" NaVante responded.

As three nurses rushed in handing the doctor some tools, which he laid on the table. He held his hand up and looked Ree-Ree in the face.

"Look, your baby has turned a great deal. If you push, it will be fatal, and if he goes any higher, it could be fatal. So you relax and be as still as you can." Doctor Wells then gave me a sorry-ass look.

I stared down at Ree-Ree, and with tears in my eyes, I watched the tears run down her face. She reached her other hand out, and NaVante took it.

I looked over, and tears were coming down NaVante's face. We were all scared and confused.

"You've always had my heart, Bigg. I love you, and all I ever wanted was to be here for our family. That's all," she cried.

Reignah yelled out in pain as they moved roughly between her legs.

I felt her pain in the pit of my stomach and in my chest. All I could see was the good in her, the way she took care of me, held me down, and made sure I was always good. She had done everything in her power to show me she was mine, and she was there for me and only me. At that moment, I knew she was wifey. She'd earned it, and I was gonna give her that life, that security.

She yelled again and began to cry harder.

"Come on, dammit! Come on and turn," the doctor yelled. "Nurse, this is not working. He's gone too far, and he's slipping."

"It's gonna be all right," NaVante said, rubbing her sister's tears. "Girl, we gonna have a ball with this baby. Buy all that cute shit we saw at Cookies in Brooklyn or that store in Newark." She tried to smile.

"Oooh, Bigg, Bigg! Navy, it hurts so bad," Reignah said. "Navy, Navy! Aaahhh, Navy. Listen, take care of my baby, PLEASE! Take care of—" Ree-Ree fell back, and her body began to jolt.

The nurse rushed to her side, and we began to move back. NaVante grabbed my hands and arm as we stared into Ree-Ree's eyes, which slowly rolled back and closed. I felt heavy as I fell back against the wall, and

NaVante fell into my arms crying. I squeezed her as I looked on at the doctor still working on Ree-Ree. He was trying to grab the baby with the forceps because he had no grip.

"God, please save my baby," I prayed.

NaVante looked up. She squeezed my hand as she watched.

Through all the blood and other fluids draining from Ree-Ree's lifeless body appeared a little head full of hair and a little brown body. His face was full of scratches and bruised, but he let out a scream that let us all know he was here.

Joy filled my heart, joy filled NaVante's heart. We hugged, and we smiled, feeling the joy of life fill the room, for a minute.

They wiped him off and handed him to me. I had to sit down because the confusion clouded my brain.

I stared down at my son and smiled, tears in my eyes. I looked over at my girl, who I was supposed to be sharing this God-given moment with, who was supposed to be sitting up exhausted and smiling as I handed her our baby, and she wasn't moving. I began to cry.

I looked back over to Ree-Ree as they pulled out her IV and lost it. "Oh my God! Oh my God! Ree-Ree! Why, mami? Why this? You can't leave me like this." I looked down at my son.

NaVante came over and put her arms around my shoulders and looked down at him crying.

"Your mom's gone, man. Who gonna take care of us now?" I asked him as if he could answer.

His eyelids began to jump. Then they lifted, and showed his eyes rolling around all over, trying to focus. He finally got them locked in on me and held his stare for a minute. Then his eyes turned and locked in on NaVante. He didn't blink, move, or cry, he just stared at her.

She stared back deep into his eyes. "I'm gonna be here for you always, and I'm gonna give you a bunch of love. Know why? Know why? 'Cause I love you. Because I love you," she said again, fighting back the tears.

They came and took the baby to clean him up and check him out.

"We'll bring him to another room. The room is two doors down, so the rest of the family can come in."

We went into the other room as everyone else came in. It was a crazy moment because everyone was sad and crying. Then, when the baby came in, it was a room full of happiness and sadness.

Shamar just sat in the chair and cried.

I patted her on the back, to try and ease the pain. She grabbed my hand and squeezed it then shook her head and cried.

The evening was long and draining. I tried to keep my composure, everyone from her moms, her brother, aunts and cousins were all acting damaged from her being gone. I knew they were going to miss her, but nobody was feeling me. This was the mother of my child, and the woman that held me down, the one I reached for to comfort me, love me, and hold me down. She was in my life every day. Now what was I going to do?

I stood staring at my son through the glass. The scratches and bruises had settled in, and his little face looked a mess. The bruises on his neck and body brought tears to my eyes. I knew he needed his mother to care for him. I needed Ree-Ree here to take care of him, to hold me and let me know things were going to be all right. I stood there lost. I was truly lost, not knowing what to do next.

I felt a hand touch my back.

"Everything's going to be okay, Bigg. I promise you. Everything will be okay." NaVante stood beside me with her arm around me.

I threw my right arm around Shamar as she approached, and my left around NaVante. I squeezed them and let out a big, "Aaahhh! I know He will not put more on me than I can bear. I know He won't."

"Believe that and you'll be okay, Bigg," NaVante said.

"Fo' sho." I shook my head. "Let's get outta here. Come back in the morning, EARLY."

"This been a muthafuckin'day. My new little cousin lost his moms and almost lost his daddy," Shamar said, running up a few steps and looking back.

I laughed. "You wasn't gonna take me away from this bitch, was ya, Shamar?"

"You pissed me off big, calling me a bitch," she said, shaking her head.

"I know. All that show is that under all that manly shit, you still a woman. You all right with me, fam," I said.

She smiled, and so did NaVante.

"So y'all following me?" I asked.

"Going to y'all house, right?" A sad look came over Shamar's face. "Well, your house."

"Yeah."

Shamar said, "I'm going back to the hotel. What you gonna do, NaVante?"

"My things are at the house. I'll be there. I can ride with you?"

"Let's go," I said, headed to my truck.

It was a long ride home. I was wondering what I was going home to. LB was with his moms. He wasn't there at the hospital, but I was gonna have to find the time and talk to him.

I was gonna have to get ten grand up, so Reignah's moms could handle everything and put her away good. All the way to the house, she was saying she wanted LB to come stay with her, but her shit ain't that big. That got me confused.

Then this bitch over here talking all that Spanish shit, and I can't understand none of it. But the first call, I knew she was talking to a dude, because her emotions were up and down. Her voice went from explaining bluntly to a sad, "*Sí, sí.*"

Then she told me she had to call her father.

As she spoke to him, I could hear him fussing. She spoke back calmly, everything in Spanish. I was mad I couldn't understand her, but it caught my attention. I wanted to learn that shit. She continued her conversation until we reached the house.

Something came completely over me, but I didn't want to hesitate, and that crying shit was over. I got out and walked to the door and opened it. The house was spotless. On the table sat her album book. I walked through the kitchen. Spotless, everything clean.

I walked upstairs past NaVante as she came inside. I looked in all the rooms, and they were clean. I sat on our bed and stared at her picture. Tears again filled my eyes.

I walked over to our son's room. She had it ready with wall-to-wall sports shit.

NaVante walked in the room.

"She was ready for him. She always said this time it was gonna be right," I said.

"And you allowed her to make it right, Bigg. My sister confided in me with everything. And the way you loved her was the right way. She had committed herself to you, and she talked about all you had been through, saying, she had never been happier or been treated better. She felt happy here, Bigg, like she had the world in her hands."

"I guess God said only He could do better," I said.

We both laughed a soft laugh.

"I'm glad you here, NaVante, for real. Thanks!"

"No problem. I got y'all," she said softly. "Oh, and call me *Navy*."

"Navy, well, good night. I'll see you in the a.m." I forced a smile.

"Good night."

I disappeared in my room. I lay on my bed and contemplated calling my mom, and my peoples. I knew, "What you gonna do?" was gonna be the question. I needed to know he was mine before anything.

They did the swab thing, and because of circumstances, they were rushing the results, and I would know tomorrow.

I picked up the phone and dialed my moms.

"Hello."

"What up, Ma?"

"What's going on, boy?"

"Ree-Ree died in labor today. Baby went back up, and she went. They messed him up, getting him out with all those tools and sh—"

"Better watch yo' mouth."

"I know, Ma. My mind gone."

"So you got a son. I got a grandson that you have to raise as a single father. Oh Lord, that is gonna be a handful. When is that girl funeral?"

"Her moms handling that."

"They paying for it?"

"No, I'ma give them ten thou."

"You can buy something good for five. Real good. Hear me?"

"Yes, Mama."

"All right, I'll see you in a couple days. Call and let me know."

"Know what?"

"You know. I know you ain't stupid two times."

"Later, old lady."

"Call me what you want, but you better listen to me."

"Love ya."

"Love you too, big head."

Chapter Sixteen

I looked at my phone. It was 10:30. I reached for my other phone and saw the missed calls. I knew I had to put some work in because Rob would be ready and on point in two days.

Needing something to wake me up, I got up and jumped in the shower. Came out and threw on my black sweats, black DCs (Air Force Ones) and white tee. The weather was muggy, extra hot for May.

I walked into the garage and realized that everything I owned reminded me of Ree-Ree, and it hurt. I sat in the Tahoe and got my bearings together and began making calls as I headed to my spot on Hampshire Lane, this apartment complex called Dove Landing that sits beside some row houses called Lake Edward West. Now the other side was where I was set up before and got caught up, but this time, I was on some other shit. I had my cousins come up from Elizabeth City and hold me down. They had their peoples coming to

Virginia Beach getting theirs, and for what I was giving it to them for, they could even show niggas love.

I came inside to see the young'uns on the Xbox and Wii. Cat and one of our other cousins was playing Wii.

"What the deal?" I asked calmly, no energy at all.

"Where you been all day?" Li'l Nate asked.

"Girl had my son," I said.

He and Cat both looked at me.

"She died, man. My boy gave her hell coming here. I never thought—"

"Sorry, man, for real," Cat said. "Nobody wants to lose their baby moms. Them hoes gotta take care of them bad muthafuckas."

We smirked slightly.

"So you do what you needed to do before you go accepting all that gotdamn responsibility?"

"What you mean, cousin?" I asked.

"Nigga, if it's yours, raise your son, if not, she's just another bitch you used to fuck wit' gone."

"Don't you got no compassion?" I asked.

"Hell naw. My momma say all that shit left Plymouth with yo' momma."

We laughed again.

"I got two peoples coming through. Tagor getting a whole joint, and Renk getting a half."

"That ain't over here. Think a half might be here," Cat said.

"Young'un, see if a half in there," Li'l Nate said.

After a sec, he returned, "Naw, 'bout ten ounces."

"Go get those last two joints from the other spot," Li'l Nate said. "Both of y'all go. We'll handle it, cuz. Go home. Regular price, right?" Li'l Nate asked me, feeling the sad news.

"Exactly. I appreciate it, fam. I got to make this move to Miami Wednesday, but I'm coming straight back. Then we should be right back before the weekend."

"Sound good. Go relax, fam. You had a day," Li'l Nate said.

"Yo, I'm out," I said, headed back out.

"Oh! Yeah, y'all niggas need to have that for me tomorrow," I said, looking at them.

Another cousin, Smalls, sat in the chair looking at the Wii game. He hadn't acknowledged me or said a word. I always felt he was a little slow, but he always stayed close to Rob.

"Then I need to head to Plymouth. I got money to get in Elizabeth City and Williamston," Li'l Nate said, referring to the small towns in NC.

"New Bern, Manteo," Cat added.

"Ahoskie. I fucks with Ahoskie. Yeah, I like that spot," Smalls said.

These were the first words out his mouth. I didn't know this little 5-5, 140-lb. little nigga could talk.

"Cuz got pussy in Ahoskie," Cat said.

"Yeah, and no bodies." Li'l Nate laughed until Smalls cut him a look, and the smirk slid off his face.

"Y'all niggas crazy. Well, after you handle that, put that up, shut it down, and go take care of that."

"Leaving young'uns here. They good," Cat said with confidence.

I headed back home, my mind relaxed as far as my business went.

I arrived back home about midnight. When I came in, I heard NaVante in the guest room talking on the phone. It sounded like fussing was going on, but the sadness in her voice let me know that the person on the other end had to mean something to be able to control her emotions.

I changed into my shorts and T-shirt and walked downstairs. I went over to my bar and poured me a double shot of Grey Goose, sat on my soft brown leather, and flipped on the 42-inch flat-screen. After finding a rap countdown on VH1, I pulled out the drawer to the coffee table and pulled out my Backwoods Cigars and Kush, the most exotic weed available on the streets of Tidewater. As I lit my "Back" and cradled my drink, I felt NaVante's presence.

"Thought your day had ended?" NaVante walked in the kitchen. She pulled the wine from the refrigerator and poured a glass then returned to the den.

"Had to see my cousin and check on something."

"Yeah, check on something," she said with a slight smirk.

"For real. In a couple days I got to be in Miami. I'm trying to figure this all out."

"Your mind is moving too fast, especially for what just happened. Try to relax your mind and see what the doctors say tomorrow about everything," she said softly, staring at me.

I stared back, my eyes pressed tight and shaking my head. It was the first time I had stared at her in the low light. With her light skin, light brown hair that blended perfectly with her light brown eyes, slim nose, and small lips, this girl looked white. I had to blink twice to get better vision.

"I hear ya, I hear ya," I said in a low tone, but loud enough for her to hear me.

She sat down next to me and reached out for the "Back." "Don't smell like no garbage," she said.

"Please. You ain't never smelled me burning no bull-shit in my house and you been here how many times?" I couldn't believe she let that come out her mouth.

She pulled on the "Back," allowing the Kush to fade into her mind. "Taste like 'piff.' It's good."

"It's Kush. I know y'all New York people got different names, but that's some exotic," I said, knowing it was my shit.

She laughed at my expressions and my Southern accent.

"It's good. I can roll with it." She smiled and stood up in her University of Maryland sweats and T-shirt.

"I forgot you graduated from Maryland."

"Yeah, I used my degree for a second, but I was getting ready to go back and get my masters, but all this has blown my mind. I can't think straight." She hit my Back once more and sipped her wine.

"I'm gonna say good night, Bigg. I needed this. My boyfriend buggin' on me after the day I had." She passed me back my "*L.*"

"He go to school in Maryland too, right? That's dude you brought to the cruise we all went on?"

"Yeah, he go to Johns Hopkins in Baltimore, thirty minutes from where I went. He'll be a doctor in two years. Our families are real proud."

"You proud too, huh? Gotta be, you wearing his ring," I said. It was really my first time noticing it.

"Yeah, he took me to the Dominican Republic and proposed in front of his family and mine for our vacation last year. I couldn't say no."

"I heard that. Got something good, lock it down." I laughed.

"That he did." She smiled. "Good night," she added and walked away with her glass of wine.

Chapter Seventeen

Fox slowly walked into the dimly lit restaurant that sat on M Street in the Georgetown section of D.C. He walked to the back and joined two older gentlemen that were about twenty-five years our senior.

"Please have a seat," the lieutenant colonel said.

"Sure, sir. What do I owe this meeting?" Fox said, trying to ease the tension he felt.

"Look at the menu. Order something, soldier," the lieutenant colonel said softly, allowing every word to slide off his tongue.

"My wife got dinner tonight, and if I don't eat, you know the problems that can cause." Fox smiled.

"Don't make a problem, when you don't have to," the other gentleman said. He was a chief on a Navy carrier that made several trips to South America on six-month deployments. He was the real link. The one that brought duffel bags of cocaine back to be distributed to the colonel in Washington and a retired DEA agent in Baltimore.

"You are so right, sir."

"Then you should agree that if a problem does occur, you handle it before it gets too big," the colonel said.

"That's right, sir."

"We heard that one of your players is in some shit and the little bitch he wit' is there to bring him down," the other gentleman said.

Fox sat quietly, looking at both men.

"The girl is the cousin of the kids that got caught up at Virginia Tech, and it trickled down to your partner in South Carolina. It's a hop, skip, and a jump from you, because the girl has found your partner and is slowly setting him up, with plans to bring him down to get her family leniency."

"Sir, we've parted from our arrangements. I don't deal with any of my past partners," Fox said, hoping it would resolve the problem, at least for the moment.

"Listen here," the chief said. "This meeting was not my idea. 'Eliminate Captain Fox and anybody that he's touched." Those were my words. How and where we get our accurate information is not your concern, but do know, we know it's accurate. You have the choice to eliminate him and the girl, or we will start from the top and execute all y'all niggas," he said under his breath.

Fox said, "Fuck you say, old man? Say it again and see me fuck you up."

"I'll beat your black ass, muthafucka," the old man said a little above a normal level.

"Calm down, calm down." The colonel patted his friend's shoulder. "Captain, you heard what was said? Handle it. Can I count on you?" He stared Fox in the eyes.

"Yes, sir," Fox said slowly, still trying to put together all that had just happened.

"All right, excuse yourself, soldier," the chief said.

Fox stared into his eyes, to find softness in the old man trying to be hard, but he could tell the words the mature gentleman spoke were for real.

He walked toward the exit in deep thought, but soon as he walked out the doors of the restaurant, he scanned the area, and became ready for whatever. He climbed into his new Cadillac Escalade truck. Business had been good, and things were finally falling into place on the distribution and sales side of things.

Fox was no longer dealing with his friends anymore, and things with his wife were still up and down. For a while he thought things were looking up, but lately she'd been withdrawing. Her flipping-out stages were becoming less frequent, but she seemed distant from time to time. She still went into deep stares, but not as if she was disturbed, but just in deep thought. She always asked him to do things as a family, more so a demand, and after the death of their son, she wouldn't make a move without him. Now she was moving around more like she was finally finding herself without him.

Fox had never felt insecure, but he needed her to want him, need him, lean on him, be dependent on him, because she was the one he depended on, leaned on, and needed so bad. And now was that time.

He had no idea he was gonna be hit with the shit that had just been thrown at him. All his shit was gonna have to change, where he lived, his family life, his business, and his connect, or lay his friend down and keep living. His mind raced as he sipped from the cup of Hennessy he had in his hand while driving.

"Call Joy," he said loud enough for his phone to dial. She didn't answer. He tried again, no answer.

"Call Erica," he said.

After two rings she picked up. "Hello," she said.

"We need to meet."

"I ain't nowhere near D.C. I'm in Delaware."

"What's going on there?"

"Girl I was stationed with in Korea lives here. We got mad close, and she been asking me to come out and check things out."

"And?" Fox asked anxiously figuring it could be a move.

"Then get on back. Something has been thrown at me, and I need to holla at you."

"That serious?" she asked.

"That serious."

"See you in three hours at the house. That good?"

"Thanks," Fox said, spaced out, his mind on his wife. He figured he would head home to see her, and that talking with her would clear his head of his family troubles.

He pulled up to his home to see his wife's car parked out front. *Why didn't she answer the phone?* he thought to himself, getting out the truck. He felt better as he opened the door and walked inside. "What's up, babe?" he said to his wife as she sat reading *O* magazine.

"Not too much. Good day," she said, seemingly in a good mood.

"So what happened with you?"

"I think I'm going back to work. I been talking to my therapist about it, and she said that it would be good. So I went by and talked to Mr. Sanomo today."

Fox looked at her with passion in his eyes but hurt in his heart for what he was about to tell her. She was the happiest he'd seen her in a long time. He looked into her slanted light brown eyes and bronze skin. He licked his lips when his eyes rested on her full lips before moving to the little mole that sat perfectly high on her left cheekbone. Her dark brown hair that was cut into layers and came back to a point like a mane and rested on her back between her shoulders completed the beautiful package. The darkness and bags around her eyes were gone, and the whiteness in her eyes showed, and when she smiled, she shined. This was the woman he married, the woman he fell in love with, and he wanted to love her and take care of her and hold her close for eternity.

"So what you thinking?" she asked, breaking the silence.

"It sounds wonderful that you can get ready to go back, and even better that your job is still there," Fox said without any real emotion.

"I've been dealing with a lot for a while. And with the help of God, church, and my therapist, my mind and body feel strong. I even went to our son gravesite," she said, looking at Fox and his reaction.

"No, you didn't."

"Yes, I did. And I stood out there and cried like I never cried before. And then I prayed and gave it to God. I know you not one who talks and gives God all the praises, but He's the only one who could truly help me help myself. Still growing, but I'm gonna be all right." She smiled.

Fox looked at his wife, and a feeling of happiness came over him for a moment.

"I met with the colonel today. He had a partner who was a chief in the Navy. I They told me that Rob girl is with him, and she's setting him up to save her cousin, that young boy that got caught up at Virginia Tech."

"How they know all this?" Joy asked, letting him know she was paying attention.

"This chief cat was real rude. Called me a nigga and all that type shit." Fox went over to his bar and poured himself some Hennessy.

"Pour me one too." Joy knew she was going to need one from the way the story started.

He handed her a glass of Cîroc, and continued as he sipped his drink. "They told me I need to eliminate Rob and his girl," he said, looking at her.

"Did you tell them that you no longer associate with him?"

"Told them. It made no difference. They said to take them out, or they were going to eliminate me and everybody I've touched. I really have no choice." Fox downed the Hennessy.

"You're not a killer. That's not what you do."

"I'm trying to figure out what to do. I'm fucked up over this shit. I'm thinking I should call a meeting with them and say something, but we broke away on not so good terms," he said with his head down. He looked up at his wife. "Maybe I should just get a team together and pay some niggas to go and handle Rob and his snitching-ass bitch."

"You handle it the way you see fit. But don't send no amateurs or pros. You better send the best, because they walking into a death trap. And if he find out you sent them, then you'll have the colonel and your team looking for you."

"Naw, I'm gonna handle it, but I was thinking that we need to move. I don't want us easily found."

Joy asked loudly, as if he was crazy, "Move where?"

"Virginia. Williamsburg."

"Sorry, baby, but this is your problem now. You go take care of it, and we'll be right here."

"No, we're going. We gonna sell the house and move. If I leave, they still can find y'all, and that's not gonna happen."

"I'm not going anywhere. I'm finally bringing my life and myself back together. I'm not going nowhere, and if I do, I'm going by myself. I didn't marry you to deal with all this shit you putting me through."

"Put you through what?"

"I married a lieutenant in the Army, not a drug-dealing drunk, capable of manslaughter. Not only manslaughter, but you killed our child," she yelled. This moving thing was the last straw. She was fed up with him.

"No. What and who you married is standing here in front of your ass," he yelled back. Joy had got him so upset, he was ready to slap her just to get her attention and make her listen to his every word, but she wasn't his child. "Look here ,Joy," he said calmly.

"No, you look here, honey. When I first started going to my sessions, my therapist suggested that we separate because I had a lot of anger and resentment towards you, but I said no, we would work through it together, like husband and wife, but it's been hard and it has become too much. We need a break, a real break, and now is a good time."

Fox stood staring at his wife. He couldn't believe what he'd just heard. Never in a million years did he think Joy would leave him. Now here she was standing in front of him saying it was over. He wanted to grab her, hold her and never let her go, to beg her not to leave him, but he'd been paralyzed by her words. He was so hurt, words wouldn't form to come out his mouth.

"Okay," he said, emotions running all through his body and aching heart.

Fox picked up his keys and walked out. He jumped in the Cadillac truck and fled to his townhouse to meet Erica. It was a long drive. He couldn't imagine his life without Joy. That would crush his world.

He sat around drinking until Erica arrived.

"What up, sir?" she said, coming in the door in her Apple Bottoms jeans and white T-shirt that stopped above her waist and showed her pierced belly button. She walked over and sat down and threw her new light blue-and-white Jordan's on the table.

Fox sat not saying a word.

"Do I need to call Butch?" she asked.

"I don't know. You been with me a long time. I seen you handle yourself in these D.C. streets like a nigga, but always carry yourself like a lady. I know you capable of the murder game. That's what I need now," he said, still trying to digest all that was going on.

"Captain, I brought Butch in because he's a brother. We are 'Blood-related.' I do what I do because I'm connected to the streets in more ways than one. We're heavy in the military, but we keep it low. Don't ask, don't tell, and don't flag. Butch is gang-related too, and when I went to Richmond with him, I found out exactly how big he was. How you think he took those six things you lost in Norfolk and Columbia with no problem? Call him?"

"Yeah," Fox said with no emotion.

Erica took out her phone and texted Butch. TOWN-HOUSE NOW, ASAP!

Fox stood up and took a deep breath. "I got a partner who made a fucked-up choice when it came to his girl. She's a snitch, and for that, they both have to go."

"Sir, I can see this decision bothers you, but remember, you can't allow nobody to destroy the lives of many. One person can't destroy people careers. You can't allow one person to destroy everybody that you are connected to like families, including your own." Erica looked at Fox dead in his eyes as she spoke.

He looked at her and wondered if she knew what he was going through with his family. "So you a Blood? How that come off?"

"Got in when I was fifteen. I was like a tomboy. I wanted to run with niggas and get money, so my brothers let me hang. I watched them bang and get money. I saw my brother Tank run niggas with fear, beat niggas' asses. Then his murder game was so treacherous, and he had fear in so many people, our whole family wanted him to get locked up, thinking prison would calm him down." Erica shook her head.

"Where's he? Locked up?" Fox smiled as if he knew.

"Naw, he fucked up. He killed some dude and robbed him. A year later, dude cousin got out and caught my brother by himself and beat the shit out of him, left him brain-dead. Nothing could be done because he was another Blood, and he did it with his hands. But I learned from him. My other brother was a slick-ass nigga, pretty boy, always got game. Always had some way to get money out a nigga. Played both sides of the fence and got caught. Nigga knew he had set him up. Dude walked up, and I was standing right beside him. Dude said, 'You got that sixty thousand you got me for in your pocket, Busta?' My brother laughed and said, 'Nigga, you crazy.' Dude pulled out a chrome .45 and blew his brains out. Guess what?"

"What?"

"I learned from that. I don't play that slick shit. Don't put shit in the game."

"What about your other one?"

"He was true to the game. Wasn't wild, wasn't slick, straight businessman, gang-related, and because of all his ties, I was blessed in and worked closely under my brother, BoJack. I never got respect. He always told me, 'Treat people with respect. Always make sure your money good. Do what you have to do. No hesitation, nothing more, nothing less.' So you mix those three, and you got Erica. Know when to wild out like Tank, know when to be slick like Busta, and always stay focused and do what I have to do like Bo." She smiled.

"So where is he at now?" Fox asked as they heard the door open.

"Lorton. Close enough if I need him," she said, quickly finishing the conversation. "What the deal, Butch?" she asked.

"You know, popping all day. How you, sir?"

"At a crossroad and need some help," Fox answered.

"You know I'm here for whatever," Butch said, anxiously wanting to know what was going on.

"One of my partners in my organization got a leech, and the leech is a snitch. Need them both executed before they bring down everything that's been built."

"Who?" Butch was hoping Sidney was their target. He owed him something.

"Rob and his girl." Fox forgot that Butch had met his team in Virginia Beach.

"But Rob was okay," Butch said. "We was dealing with him after all the bullshit. He didn't seem like—"

"What a snitch look like?" Fox asked.

"Sir, I will do whatever you say. I questioned it because this is your man, your family, and once in motion, a man don't come back from the dead," Butch said, putting an emphasis on dead.

Fox went into a deep stare, that was his very reason for feeling so funny, Rob was his man, longtime friend, his family and he knew Rob wouldn't tell shit, he couldn't, he was on the run, but being with that bitch was the wrong choice. Now he had to suffer with her.

"Location is Miami. I will narrow it down in a few days. Target is Rob and the girl, Reignah."

"I got some peoples in Atlanta that will handle it, sir. Five thousand a head."

"I told him we were united by Blood," Erica said looking at Butch.

Butch looked at Fox.

"Use your resources, but they better be good, or it's suicide," Fox explained.

Butch looked at Fox. "Oh! He out of Fort Bragg too? He a eighty-second Airborne Paratrooper?"

"With Green Beret training, Special Ops training, he a fighting muthafucka, and he hell with guns," Fox said.

"I got you. I need to make a call to Bad Newz," Butch said. "That call is twenty thousand a head, but these cats are military-trained mercenaries out of Fort Eustis. They been out, but they live in Newport News. They live off making hits anywhere in the country and abroad," Butch said, co-signing his people's work.

"You know of these guys firsthand?" Fox asked.

"Firsthand, sir," Butch said, no smile, no expression.

"Bring me eighty thou, and hold forty thou for the job." Fox knew Butch had gotten six kilos of cocaine at twenty thousand apiece and was supposed to bring back one hundred twenty grand, so he said bring eighty and call it even.

"Done," Butch said.

"Well, I'm gonna be out. I'll catch up with y'all tomorrow. And I'll try and get more information, so it will narrow your search. This is a done deal," Fox said, easing toward the door.

Fox drove home in silence. No music played to soothe his mind after his long, stressful day. Only the sound of the wind blowing across the window. He drove at 50 on the 55 mph road, his mind in deep thought.

He went back to his college days, where his friends went in the military as enlisted. He wanted to do better, so he took the long road and went to college, got into ROTC, and got commissioned into the same Army as his friends, but as an officer, total different class. He was on top of the world. Then came the alcohol, then criminal charges, then discharged from what he worked so hard for, and then to the streets. His wife was right. He didn't even know how the hell he got where he was.

He remembered pulling his friends into this drug world, something they knew nothing about, but he slowly showed them how to take full advantage of being friends with someone well connected. Now here he was plotting to kill his lifelong friend.

He pictured Rob in his mind, then Bigg, Bink, and Sidney all playing at the park. A pain shot through his chest, and his stomach turned. He took a deep breath, and his eyes filled with tears, but he refused to let them fall.

As he got off at his exit, thoughts of Joy being gone pulled at his heart. He pictured an empty home. He pulled over and threw his hands over his face. He let out a deafening growl. "Aaaghh! What the fuck!" he said loudly.

He wiped his face and headed home. He walked through the door, and no bags were at the door.

He went to the bedroom. There, Joy lay balled up under the beautiful comforter. He undressed and slid in bed behind her. He took her in his arms and squeezed her. "I'm taking care of everything. We won't have to go nowhere," he said in her ear.

Joy rolled over and faced him, took him in her arms, and held him.

Fox felt so tired and drained, but so secure, that he fell fast asleep.

Chapter Eighteen

June 2006

"Look at my boy. He's live now. Look at him trying to lift his little muthafuckin' head." I laughed.

"Shut up!" NaVante said! "He's a doll with all that hair on his head." She smiled.

"Nigga ain't no doll. Little muthafuckin' man," Shamar added. "Yo, I been down here almost a week. I gots to get back to Jersey. So when they say Basan coming home?"

"Tuesday. I hope he's healthy enough. I been praying. Lord let me take my nephew home," NaVante said.

"For real, I'm ready to get him home," I said. "Looking like a gotdamn Dominican with that slick-ass hair."

"That's Daddy coming out," NaVante said.

"That look like Masso," Shamar said, referring to Ree-Ree's and Navy's father.

"You seen pictures of your father?" I asked out of curiosity. I had never seen any pictures that Ree-Ree might have had around.

"Pictures? I go see my dad at least twice a year in the

Dominican Republic. Shamar been a couple times," NaVante said.

"I heard that," I said.

"I'm gonna send him pictures after we get him home and dress him in some of those cute things Ree-Ree brought." NaVante's expression changed.

"It'll be okay. You gonna hold Ree down, you gonna be a real auntie slash godmother, and I feel you," Shamar said.

NaVante hugged her cousin, and they cried again.

The emotions crowded the hall, and my eyes watered. But I had shed my last tear. It was time to pull myself together. I had to remind myself that I was a man and a Marine. I was to handle everything with my head up and my vision clear.

"So when is the funeral?" Shamar asked.

"Monday," I answered. "Her moms said the wake was Sunday."

"Well, I'm getting ready to roll out. I'll be back Sunday. What you gonna do, Navy?" Shamar asked.

"Huh?" I looked at NaVante. I realized she was my crutch, and I was leaning on her presence for comfort.

She looked back at me and stared with her lips slightly parted, as if waiting for me to give her a reason to stay.

"I might need to go and get some more things. I want to stay a couple weeks when Basan come home, and I have nothing here for a funeral," NaVante said, giving her reason for having to go home. "You make sure you get up every day and get up here and check on him early, Bigg!" She smiled. "Tomorrow, Saturday, and Sunday. Don't play. Your son gonna be looking for you."

"He gonna be looking for auntie. She was up early and out. I couldn't get up."

"I'm gonna go crazy thinking about him."

"Know what? I'm supposed to go to Miami tonight. It's a must, and I plan to get back tomorrow. Can't stop this money. Navy, if you stick around, I would really appreciate it." I was praying she could see that I was in desperate need of her presence at this time in my life.

"Okay, I got you," she said in a joyful manner.

"Thanks," I said, and we hugged.

"Well, I'm outta here. You good, Navy?" Shamar asked.

"I'm good, girl. Get outta here," NaVante said, fanning her cousin off.

"Be safe, Bigg. You all that little nigga got. He need you here, out here." Shamar gave me a pound and walked out the doors.

"You ready?" I asked.

"Yes," she said, and we walked out headed to the house.

We weren't at the house twenty minutes, and I was out, headed up 58 toward 85S. Leaving NaVante to watch over my home and my son left me asking myself how I put so much trust in a woman I barely knew, and it wasn't because Ree-Ree had co-signed for her.

I rode down 85 in deep thought. The loss of my girl bothered me, but I had to start concentrating on taking care of my boy. I was glad NaVante had stepped up and was helping me out a great deal. She was there while the doctors talked to me, letting me know each and every thing that was going on with Basan. I was thankful for the extra ears and hands. I needed them.

Just then my phone rang. "What's up, partner?" I was actually happy my boy was calling. We'd decided to meet in Atlanta, instead of him driving all the way to Fayetteville.

"I'm on seventy-five and making good time," Rob said.

I actually believed the thrill of this game gave him energy. Whenever he was in the tight spots, he got hyped. What him and Carol Anne had in the trunk could take him and her off the street for life.

"I'm almost to eighty-five, coming through Emporia now," I said, looking around.

"Be careful coming through there. That's a state trap for Virginia." He laughed.

"No doubt. I'm taking it easy. Got my mind on the ATL. I been fucked up, Rob. Got some real talk when I see ya," I said seriously.

"All right, all right, but Carol Anne said you got some business," Rob said, hyping the situation. "Here she go."

"What the deal, honey?" she asked in her white voice that sounded black, but sexy in its own way.

"Everything's good, babe, always," I said in a regular tone, so she couldn't figure out my mood.

"Getting a little scarce lately. You don't like this Miami love?" she asked softly and in a pouting way.

"Love Miami and all the love it got to offer, you know that," I said coming at her.

"Then act like it. Let me see."

Rob yelled, "Let me see what? Huh!" He was laughing, trying to be funny. "Yo, homie, y'all crazy. I'll check you in nine hours."

Eight hours later, I rolled up to a hotel by Lenox Mall in the Buckhead section of Atlanta and checked into the Marriott. I got two adjoining rooms.

Rob and Anne arrived two hours later. They came up, and I gave Rob his key to the adjoining room. He gave me my packages, and I gave him the money for re-up. After we put everything up and out the way, we sat down to roll up some of that haze my man had brought me from "the Bottom."

"So we on that side?" Carol Anne asked.

"Yeah."

"Y'all finish talking. I'm gonna go get a shower and relax for a few," she said to me softly. She shut the ad-joining door, leaving me and Rob to talk.

"So what's so serious?" Rob asked.

"Ree-Ree gave birth to my son, Basan." I stared at him. "And don't ask. I already had a blood test—ninety-nine point eight percent."

"Congratulations, Bigg, for real," he said giving me a pound and passing me the haze-filled Dutch.

I usually would have turned down a Dutch, but it was filled with haze. "Thanks, man, but Ree-Ree died in the process. I lost my baby momma son."

"Damn! Damn, man! Now that's fucked up. Shorty was there for ya. I saw how she held you down while you was fucked up and scared to get this money."

"Nigga, I wasn't scared," I said, trying to save face.

"Bigg, you was fucked up and shook. Ree-Ree nursed you back to your feet then slowly let you see you needed and wanted more. Then she helped ease you back in. I know she was your crutch for a while. How you hold-ing up?"

"I'm good. Just dealing with it and trying to figure out my next move," I said, going into a stare and pass-ing back the Dutch.

"Get this money. Take care of your boy. You got to raise him, man. I fucked up my shit, and any chance of a family." Rob, his head down, pulled hard on the Dutch. "I'm on the run. If they see me and know me anywhere, it's on, baby." He shook his head. "So your man coming to help you out?"

"Naw, he come home Tuesday. Ree-Ree funeral Monday."

"So you gonna try and do it yourself, or you gonna get a nurse?"

"Well, right now Ree-Ree sister been there like that. She was in the room with me the whole entire time holding her other hand. She came in from Jersey and been there. She there now, while I'm here. Nice girl."

"That's all right. You ain't by yourself."

"She only staying two weeks then she out." I was gonna have a life-changing role coming up.

"I didn't even know Ree-Ree had sisters. Damn! So what she look like?"

"I ain't even gonna front, Rob. I ain't even looking at her like that."

"Where she been staying?" he asked.

"At the house, guest room, same room she was in when Ree-Ree let her come in," I said with attitude.

"She smoke?"

"Yeah!"

"She drink?"

"Wine," I said.

"Nigga, please . . . Wine get them hoes fucked up. She got a man?"

"Yeah! Dude a doctor, going to college in Baltimore," I said.

"Nigga ain't shit. He in school, he a college student." Rob laughed. "He ain't no doctor yet. Yo, Bigg, look at me." He patted me on my leg and stared me down.

"We been friends forever, brothers, soldiers. Don't fuckin' blink. What color is her hair?"

"Light brown," I answered.

"What color is her skin?"

"Light brown."

"What color are her eyes, Bigg?" Rob asked slowly.

I pictured NaVante. "Brown?"

"Is she big, Bigg? What size is she? Large or extra large?" He laughed.

I smiled. "She's a medium."

"What? Thirty-six D?"

"No, C," I said, laughing.

"Thirty-four waist?" He laughed.

"No, twenty-six." I said smiling.

"Thirty-six ass, Bigg?" Rob asked hype.

"Thirty-eight. Phatter than norm." I had fallen into his game.

"She sound nice. What's wrong? She got weave? She got fucked-up teeth?"

"Naw, no weave. Pretty white teeth and a slamming smile," I said, fucking with Rob.

"Is she black?"

"Dominican."

"Damn! She speak that shit?" Rob smiled.

"All the time on the phone."

"Is she fine or what, Bigg? She sound bad as shit. I know she can't fuck with Reignah." Rob looked at me.

"She's beautiful, Rob. Bad is an understatement. She is beautiful."

"So you sit around at night with her, just you and her, smoking haze, sipping alcohol in night clothes, and you don't be ready to fuck? Come on, Bigg. This me," he said seriously.

"Rob, I raise my hand to God. I've noticed her beauty, but I've been fucked up inside, hurting. I have never looked at her or hugged her or thought or felt I wanted to fuck her. For real."

"Well, it's like this. If she stay two weeks and take care of your son like his mother would, then you'll be a fool to let her leave. Do she got sense? What she do?"

"I don't know. She got a degree from the University of Maryland."

"Bigg, on the serious side, Ree-Ree was good to you, but she gone. After the funeral Monday, she is your past. Tuesday, you and your future will go pick up your son, and you got two weeks for her to realize she need to be there."

"That's her sister. That's Ree-Ree sister," I said. "That shit ain't right."

"If it make you happy and she happy, who the fuck can it hurt? Huh?"

I stared at him. "Everyone involved."

"And who's involved? Ree-Ree can't be hurt, and if your son aunt step up and raise him like her son, who's that bad for? I'm just asking."

"We jumping the gun. This my life. She got her life, and I'm gonna appreciate the support until it's gone. I ain't fuckin' with that girl sister," I said, thinking she wouldn't give up a doctor for a street soldier.

"Bigg, I love you, man, and I feel your situation. And I don't want you to be alone. But when you get home Tuesday morning, when you get up and go pick up Basan, ask yourself this. Why go out and look for a new girl when you got the perfect woman already caring for your family and already living in your home?" Rob smiled.

I smirked at my longtime friend, and all his advice for me like he was an old head.

After we'd been talking about forty-five minutes, I stood to go to my room. Then it hit me that I hadn't asked about Reignah.

"So what's going on with your girl? She ain't working with the feds, is she?" I laughed.

"They ain't came and got me yet," he said, laughing.

"So y'all good?"

"I bought a house out in the Marimar, North Miami
in Broward County. Real nice shit. She's pregnant,
man," he said with a smile.

"That's all right. Congrats."

"Thanks! I been making moves around Miami too,
man. That's another reason I wanted to get away from
down there and just use the house for holding and
moving. I got two new prospects that's trying to get me
to buy from them, some other Haitians, and some niggas from Coral City."

"Rob, we good. Stick with the cat we dealing with.
His prices are good and plus if we holla at Wyi-Z, he
should be coming down on shit now. We been dealing
with him a while, and now we burying ten kilos at a
time, straight up, and he still charging sixteen thousand five hundred. That's bullshit, you trying to go
around him, when you should be going straight at him.
Check it. I'm gonna take this back then I'm gonna fly
down there and talk to him before we buy again."

"You got too much on your plate right now. I'm
down there, and I'm gonna talk to him. Because, you
right, sixteen and a half is too high, especially for as
long as this been going on. I got you," he said, relaxing
my mind.

*For Wyi-Z to come down to at least fourteen grand
would really put a brother up*, I thought. "So you
gonna put your peoples on hold until you talk with
Wyi-Z then we go from there?"

"Exactly."

"So what's with shorty peoples?" I asked, concerned.

"One still locked up, and the other one is in Charlotte. He went there and set shit up quick, doing his thing like he always had."

"You serve him?"

"Believe it or not, I love my girl, but I let her go and meet him. She met him in Orlando, and they did their thing, and she brought it back. Money always good. She holding me down. I love the hell out of her, Bigg. She with me. Ain't no way she working with the feds."

I believed him. "Well, you better be careful, you got a baby coming in this world and you got to be here to raise him too."

"No doubt," he said. "Gonna chill for a minute then I'm hitting the strip club."

"You live in Miami. No better strip clubs," I said.

"No, the bitches are the finest in the world, but Atlanta got the phattest Black bitches with crazy bodies. That's what I'm looking for tonight. You gotta come. You need to come. Check you in a bit," he said.

I made my way through the connecting room door and locked it. I turned around to find Carol Anne lying in the middle of the bed with a turquoise lace set on, the bra laced in white, and panties with a little white bow on the front.

I went over and pulled her panties off and put my face between her legs and began licking her. I licked her lips then the inside, darting my tongue in and out, up and down, around and around for about fifteen minutes, never touching her clit.

She begged me to lick it. "Please, please?"

I brought my tongue up across her hole and licked her clit, and she jumped. By the time her butt hit the bed, I had her clit locked between my lips, sucking and pulling softly until her clit emerged from its shell. I flickered it with my tongue as I sucked harder.

Her legs open, and her back arched, she let out a loud "Aaaaaghhh!" Then she forced my head from between her legs and rolled over in a ball.

She lay there for about ten minutes as I contemplated getting up, until I felt her hand around my "servicer." As he swelled in her hands, she eased down and faced him. She licked the head quickly with her tongue over and over, but never put it in her mouth. Then she licked it up and down, around and around, balls and all. Then she ran her tongue from the bottom to top for about fifteen minutes, until my dick kept jumping,

But she never did til I said, "Please, please, get it out, please."

Then she started from under my balls and took a long, slow lick up my shaft to the tip then quickly took the head in her mouth and sucked softly, with a lot of suction.

I almost screamed from the wet feeling of her mouth on my happiness. When I thought I was in heaven, I felt her tongue slowly go across the head and around it. I tensed up, and grabbed the back of her neck and pushed it into her throat and let it all go. And she took it all and never gagged, leaving me empty.

She kept sucking, and I tried to push her off, but she gripped my dick and squeezed it as she held on and kept sucking. I threw my hands up and balled my fist, trying to fight the sensation running through my body, which shook and jolted as she forced me to deal with it and get back.

Minutes later, my dick was rock-hard and ready to

go. I laid her back and entered her as she opened wide, grabbed the back of her knees, and pulled her legs back, allowing me to get all I wanted.

And when I came, it felt as if all the bullshit that filled my mind and body came shooting out, and my body collapsed. She lay flat on her stomach, gasping for air, glad I finally came.

I jumped in the shower and came out to find her in the same spot, same position, except now I didn't have to wonder if she was dead because of the loud snores that filled the room.

I threw on my True Religion jeans with my black Prada and my black tee. I opened the connecting door to see Rob sitting, pulling on another Dutch. I came in and hit it.

"You ready?" I asked.

"Fuck, yeah! Let's go," he said, heading for the door.

I opened the connecting door and told him to stop. "Look at my work!" I said, staring at Carol Anne.

Rob took two steps back and looked. "Yeah! You do good work. She snoring, out cold. Don't even know we standing here looking at her naked, sexy ass." He laughed.

I shut and locked the connecting door then went out the front.

We went over to Magic City and blew about a gee in VIP. Rob, about $3500 in the Gold Room. We stayed til around 3:00 a.m. then called it a night.

Chapter Nineteen

The next morning him and Carol Anne climbed in her new Camry and headed back to Miami. I climbed in my '98 Maxima I used for road trips and headed back up 85 North.

It was ten when I left and eight when I turned into the complex with the house I owned out the beach. I pulled in the garage and put up three bricks and moved two to the townhouse so Li'l Nate and Cat could have access. I left there and went by the hospital to see my boy.

It was Friday night about 10:00 p.m., and my mind and body was finally slowing down as I stood staring at my boy sleeping in a bubble with little patches of wires connected to him to monitor his every change. I prayed for my boy, and for God to give me strength and knowledge to raise him right without a mother. I knew the challenge he would have, not having that unconditional motherly love, but I would do all I could, to the best of my ability, to give him all he needed.

After seeing my boy, I knew the day was over. I felt totally relaxed.

I went on home and entered. The alarm was set just like I showed NaVante. The sounds of me entering must have wakened her.

I rolled a Backwoods and lit it as I leaned back on the couch, allowing the haze to fill the room.

"So you made it back safely, I see," she said, walking up with a pair of silk burgundy pajama shorts and a tank top.

I could see her breast jiggle with every movement. "Yes, I'm safe." I smiled, holding out the "Back."

"Good, good! Basan doing better each day. The doctor went over his chart with me. I'm so thankful." She put her well-manicured hand over her heart.

"You thankful? That's the first stop I made when I got back. I just left the hospital. Come on, that's my man. Don't nothing else in this world belong to me. Nothing and nobody. Got to make sure he okay."

"I'm sure you will. I truly believe that." NaVante handed me the Backwoods. "Tomorrow I'm gonna go over there early, because my boyfriend supposed to leave Baltimore at six o'clock. He said he'll be here by ten. He gonna stay til Sunday, so we got a room. I'll catch back up with you before the wake."

"Okay. That a work." I smiled.

"What you smiling about?"

"I'm just glad you been here to help me through this rough time. You are greatly appreciated," I said to her in a nice, cordial way.

"You welcome, but I'm pulling the same support from you. So thank you."

"No problem."

I laid the Backwoods in the ashtray and hit the lights, she set the alarm, and we walked upstairs.

The following morning I woke about ten a.m. Na-Vante was already gone. I looked in the garage to see the Lex still parked. I guess her boyfriend picked her up. I went and got in the shower. I got myself well groomed and pulled out some gear for the day—Antik jeans, Navy blue Wallabees, and fresh white tee. I peeped the style in the floor-length mirror.

I gathered my accessories, Cartier watch, with the Cartier diamond bracelet, my wallet, $500 for the right front pocket and $5,000 in hundreds for the left front pocket. These days my money was straight, business was straight. It was just my situation, my personal shit, that was all over the place.

I headed out the door and jumped in the truck and drove up on Virginia Beach Boulevard to S&S Car Wash and got the truck clean inside and out. Took it home and then got the Lex. Ree-Ree had mad shit inside.

After going through everything and throwing most of it away, I jumped in the Lex and shot up by the car wash, where all the ballers go get their cars cleaned. I went inside Military Circle while I waited on the car.

Afterwards I went to the hospital. It was damn near one o'clock, and NaVante was still here with her boyfriend, who was sitting patiently in the waiting area on the maternity ward.

"What are you still doing here?" I said, walking up behind her.

When she turned, I greeted her with a smile, and she greeted me with a big hug as if she was glad to see me, which was unusual. She didn't have the same bright smile or jovial attitude.

"I came about eight this morning. Then we went and had breakfast and checked into the Sheraton Waterside. We stayed there about an hour, but I couldn't get my mind off Basan, like he mine," she said.

"But he not yours. Get that in your fuckin' head." Her boyfriend stood up. Obviously, he was listening to our every word.

Her head fell at his blistering comment. "You remember Bigg?" she said, introducing me to her man.

"Yeah, I remember him," he said nonchalantly.

"Bigg, you remember my boyfriend Dominicia?" she said, keeping things cool.

The way he came at her kind of rubbed me wrong because she had been there for me. "Naw! I don't remember," I said, staring him down.

"How you?" I moved close, sticking my hand out, giving him no choice but to shake. Then I turned my body and attention back to his girl. "I'm here now. You better go and hang out while your boy in town," I said, staring at her.

"Yeah, let's do that. Told you I was only here for a day. She act like she pushed him out. We know that ain't happening."

NaVante shot him a cutting look.

"She ain't push him out, but she been here since he came into this world. I even think he raises his head and looks for her after a week of seeing her face every morning and all day," I said, smiling at her and talking to him.

"Well, I think you might need to get a nurse," he said, "because I don't think she gonna stay much longer. You can afford a nurse. Or do you need some assistance?"

"Naw, I'm good, but if you got something in your pocket, I'll take it." I stared him down, not blinking.

He blinked and looked down then back at me. When he looked down, I saw the bitch in him. He didn't want to talk to me, he just wanted to belittle her.

"No, I don't have nothing, but a number for you to call."

"No. I was asking if you had any money in your pocket. If you did, I wanted it." I smiled.

"Shit!" He smirked. "You can't get my money."

I stepped closer to him and invaded his space. "No, you missed what I said. I said if you got anything in your pocket, you don't have to give it to me, I would take it. I'll snatch you up, slam you down, rip off your pockets, and take it. You want me to show you." I was standing face to face with him.

He didn't say a word. He was shook. I had just showed his girl that he got bitch in him. He knew I had punked his ass, so I was done.

I laughed a fake laugh. "Gotcha, Dominicia," I said, pointing at him and laughing. "I'm a jokester, man. You take it easy. Don't get mad. I was just playing." I looked at NaVante for a few seconds and just turned my head and walked off.

I stayed at the hospital for a bit, sitting there in deep thought, staring at Basan. So many things flashed before me, but I knew I had to brings things together and depend on no one. I spoke to one of the nurses to see if I could hire a nurse to come by for so many hours a day to watch over my boy.

In a minute, I had set up a schedule. It was gonna be tough, but I could and would adapt to the situation.

My phone began ringing. Most of the hustlers I was dealing with before, serving them quarters, halves, and ounces hand to hand, I no longer dealt with. I gave them Cat's number, and he served them, mostly out of Dove Landing. With eight tenants in a building, traffic could roll all day. I left the hospital to head over there.

I got over there, and niggas were hanging out playing Wii. They had the bowling up, and I was just in time. I smoked, drank, and played games, at the same time trying to deal with being alone.

I missed having someone to share everything with, so I smoked more and drank more, and by the evening, I was already done.

I was gonna go back by the hospital, but I carried my ass home and laid down. No sooner than my body hit the couch, my phone rang.

"Heah, Bigg," the sweet voice carried through the phone. "This NaVante."

"You okay?"

"Yes, I'm fine. How's my man?"

"I'm okay. Little fucked up, thinking about the wake and this funeral," I said, slurring my words. "You having a good time? Enjoying Virginia Beach?"

"Okay, I'll talk to you about that later. Is Basan doing okay? Any change?"

"They said he's coming off the monitoring machine tomorrow. I didn't get back there this evening. Maybe tonight. That's who you called your man?" I fell out laughing. At first, I thought she was talking to me.

"Know what, Bigg . . . that's why I let you talk. You get fucked up and be going. I ain't pay you no attention. I was just gonna ask again in a minute," she said, a smirk in her voice.

"Just work with me. I'll be okay," I said in a joking way.

"Got you, *papi*. I might see you later. My boyfriend got mad attitude with me and won't tell me why, and he keeps badgering me. I'm dealing with so much. I don't need this right now. He went down to the bar. We gonna talk when he comes back. He might be real mad at me," she said sadly.

"You have a home to come to. Me and my son's doors are always open to you. And if they not open, I gave you a key and the security codes," I said, laughing slightly.

"That's so sweet," she said, blushing. "Thanks, Bigg."

"All right. Try to enjoy your evening, and you know where we at. Later."

Chapter Twenty

Rob stood behind the grill looking at Reignah, Blush, Carol Anne, Karen, and three other soldiers from Bragg that came to Miami and crashed at the crib. No hotel fee made for a wonderful vacation. Blush was a friend of Reignah's, and Karen and the three guys were all 82nd also. The music played, and food was cooked, and cooking. And it was more beer and liquor than everyone could drink.

Reignah and Blush sat talking more to themselves. Their conversation was South Beach, Miami, clubs, and VIP parties. The others talked about the military, wars, jumping out of planes, and where they been, which happened to be all over the world.

Everybody ate and drank until they began to slowly disperse as the hours got later.

Rob and Reignah were alone and cleaning up now. He eased behind her and put his arms around her stomach and rubbed it.

She smiled at his very touch, the feeling of his baby

growing inside of her made her melt into his arms. When she'd first arrived so much tension filled the air, but as the days went on, a lot of talking was done, hearts were mended, and eyes were opened, and their love had the opportunity to shine on them again.

When Reignah told Rob of the deal the feds were trying to pull her into, she thought he would run away from her forever. She had floated through two states before coming to Miami.

Rob knew even if she tried to avoid them, she couldn't, and they would eventually track her down, so she never worked, never used her name or credit. She was moving like him, with no existence, just the new person she'd become. She had no complaints because she was being showed love, and she wanted for nothing.

He hit the lights, walking behind her to the back room of the three-bedroom ranch ready for love.

"Let me shower first. You need to also. Smelling like charcoal, smoke, beer, and sweat don't make for a turn on." She smiled.

"I don't give a fuck what da dick smell like." Rob laughed as they undressed and headed toward the shower.

They lit candles and held each other, buried each other with hugs and kisses. Rob always told her since she'd been back that he would shower her with love. Now that she was back in his life, he would show her nothing but love.

The water began to turn cold, so they eased out the shower. Talking, touching, and drying each other off took about twenty minutes, leaving the bathroom more steamy than the hot water.

Rob opened the door to exit with a big smile, happier than he'd ever been, but the crowbar that came across his face, breaking his nose, cracking his teeth and lips, and leaving a gash in his head, from which blood poured down his face, dropped him to his knees.

Before he could get his bearings, he felt his hands and feet being bound. He looked up and saw Reignah's naked body kicking as she was being dragged across the floor from the bathroom to the den. He saw her trying to yell, but her wide eyes and open mouth with no sound let him know she was terrified.

The 6-2, 250-lb. monster had Reignah by her hair and lifted her to her feet.

Rob huffed vigorously as he watched the other 6-foot monster grab Reignah by her throat and lift her off her feet.

"Where the dough at man? Only asking once. We outta here in two minutes with money or your life."

"Ain't no money—"

Before Rob could finish his sentence, the monster lifted Reignah off her feet and slammed her to the hardwood floor on her back with such force that she lost consciousness.

Rob's heart dropped to his stomach. He stared into the monster's eyes, without any emotions. He strained to break loose, but it was useless. These weren't amateurs. And he could see, the way they were moving, money wasn't their concern.

"I'm gonna ask one more time." The 6-2 monster grabbed Reignah by the hair and lifted her up so she was sitting up. He pulled out the 9 mm with the silencer.

Rob choked on the lump in his throat as he watched the monster pull the trigger and blow her brains onto the hardwood floor.

"Fuck that bitch, nigga! She was setting your ass up.

Fox said let you live, but Butch said twenty grand for your ass." The 6-foot monster pointed his .45 at Rob and pulled the trigger, but it was on safe.

At that split second, he saw Carol Anne ease inside. They'd never given thought to the second apartment in the back. But the sound of the 9 mm with no silencer lit up the room as she took three shots, one to the 6-2 monster's head then two to the heart of the 6-foot dude that stood over Rob.

Carol Anne cut Rob loose, and in sixty seconds they had the coke and money in the Camry and Magnum and disappeared into the Miami streets.

Rob was making his way up Miami Avenue, fleeing the scene of one of the most mind-blowing things he'd ever seen. He made the left on 183rd and went from zero to 80 in seconds. He almost forgot that Carol Anne was following behind him, but she was giving her new Camry all it could take and wasn't far behind.

They saw Dade County unmarked cars and Miami Police flying past as they made their way toward Interstate 95. Rob took the exit 95N toward Fort Lauderdale. The Magnum never slowed as he hit the curve doing 90, but the 20-inch high-performance tires never made a screech.

The Camry, tight on his ass, screeched and screamed, but she never let up, and neither did the Camry.

Rob was running 120 mph up 95N before he realized he had coke in the back along with guns. *If the police pull me over now*, he thought as he ran past the Charger that had *State Police* on the side. "Ooh shit! Fuck me! Fuck me!" he yelled. His entire world had crumbled down. He looked in his rear mirror and saw the Camry a little ways back and dropping. Then he saw the flashing lights on the Charger, which was coming strong.

Rob knew he couldn't get locked up. This was do-or-die. He started to punch it, but he saw the sign *Fort Lauderdale/Hollywood Airport 6 miles*. Mad police patrolled the airport, so he began to slow down as he speed-dialed Carol Anne.

"Yeah," she answered, hyped.

"Go past the airport and take the exit into Fort Lauderdale on the right to Bob's Storage, storage one eighty-three and one eighty-four."

"Okay."

She knew it was no time for questions. She slowed down as the state police flew past her pushing 140 mph. She kept slowing until she was doing 40 in a 55 zone.

She wondered what went wrong at the house. She had no choice. She couldn't watch a soldier get killed in Afghanistan. The hell if she was gonna let that happen in her house. She now knew she was knee-deep in this shit, and it wasn't shit her mind couldn't handle. She'd seen many soldiers, people, and all likes die tragic deaths, but she cared for Bigg and Rob, so it was also personal.

"I'm a paratrooper, and I will never see my fellow soldier down. These weak-ass muthafuckas don't know what we went through over there. Leave us the fuck alone," she said making her way up 95.

Rob came to a stop, and the Charger pulled up behind him quickly. Rob had pushed all the shit in the back on the floor, except the .45 he held tight under his right leg, where the butt of the gun was in an easy gripping position.

The officer exited his Charger and approached the tinted-out Magnum. He became more alert when the window came down and he saw Rob's face. "What happened to you, sir?" he asked. "Where you coming from?"

Rob had leaned over and opened the glove compartment and got the registration and gripped the .45 that sat loaded, off safety, one in the chamber, under his thigh.

When Rob came around and stuck out the registration card, the officer's eyes widened in fright, just like Reignah's eyes a few hours ago.

Just when he was getting ready to let one go and put the officer to rest, a big *Boom*! hit the side of the Magnum. Rob jumped, not just from the collision, but also from the officer's body slamming up against the car then being twisted beyond belief and being thrown several feet in front of the car.

Rob backed up and took off after the Camry that had just done all that damage. He got in front of her, racing his way to the exit, and she followed.

He went back to the two storage units and opened them. He drove his Magnum inside one and locked it up. He pulled out the platinum S500 with a slight tint. She pulled her Camry in and locked it up, put the contents from the other vehicle under the back seat.

Rob hit the highway to 75 and went back to Atlanta, not by choice this time. Miami was a thing of the past. He and Carol Anne drove in silence. Then Rob took out his phone and dialed his man.

"What up, man? You ready already?"

"Naw, halfway through," Rob said. "They killed her, man. Those Haitians got her, man. They killed her in front of me," Rob said, as if he was in a state of shock. "I'm gonna finish this tonight. Then I'm gonna head up that way. Bigg, you talk to Fox?"

"Naw. Nigga doing his thing," I said. "You know we ain't on the best terms right now."

"Tell him you want to holla. I fucked up with the Haitians, and they came to get me. I'm on the road. I'm coming that way. We gonna straighten Fox and start fuckin' with him," Rob said. "We been apart too long. Bring it all together in Virginia."

"That's on you. You and Fox ain't have no problems," I said, not knowing what this was about.

"Set it up for Sunday night. I should be there about nine," Rob said, not knowing if I had something going with Fox, but I thought he planned on finding out.

"All right, Sunday." I wondered why he changed up. I knew those Haitians we were dealing with wasn't no joke, so if they came at him on their turf, with the artillery they got, I didn't know if Rob could have made it.

I called Fox and told him the story. How Rob was trying to play the Haitians and that shit caught up with him, and now he was leaving Miami to try and start new. He said to meet in Virginia. I felt something as Fox sat on the other end disturbed, but he was glad Rob had no idea it was him.

Fox agreed to the meeting. He was gonna get the money owed to him and get his peoples buying again.

I called Rob again.

"Yeah," he answered.

"He said, see you tomorrow night. He probably got in earlier than you," I said.

"I'll be there," Rob said sadly.

"Be safe, partner."

"No doubt, partner."

Chapter Twenty-one

Rob was feeling betrayed. Everything went through his mind as if Bigg was involved somehow. All he knew was, somebody was gonna pay for Reignah's death. He was finally happy and felt he'd found the one woman he could truly build a family with. Now he was seeing her murder play over and over.

First, the way her body was slammed, then the brain matter that flew out her head when she got hit with the .45 made his body cringe. This was real. She was never coming back. This time Reignah was truly gone, and because this motherfucking nigga said she was a snitch and wanted us dead. He wanted to snap. The anger rose so high in his head, it felt like it was gonna explode. His stomach was turning flips, making him feel sick, and his heart felt so heavy.

He squeezed his fist as tight as he could and held it as he gritted his teeth and strained with his eyes shut and head down. He allowed the pain to take over and cried briefly. He saw the look of terror in her eyes as she stared at him to save her, while he lay fucked up and bounded.

He reached up and pulled down the visor and looked at himself in the mirror. His eyes were bloodshot from the straining. A big knot and gash lay across his forehead. He couldn't really breathe good, so he thought his nose was broken, but his lip and cracked tooth still ached. And now his adrenaline had slowed down, he was really feeling some pain.

He pushed up the mirror because, looking at himself in the mirror, he felt disgusted, but he had to get it together and think it through because, at that moment, he didn't know where he was going, what he was gonna do, or his next move, which had to be crucial.

He smirked at himself as he thought about how this strategic shit was always Fox's job in their crew. Now here he was strategizing against his old friend.

"Thanks, Carol Anne," he said out the blue, realizing all she'd done. He owed his life to her.

"You wouldn't say thanks on the battlefield, soldier, and I have realized from being around you, and actually being with Bigg, that y'all are running around making the world y'all live in and grounds you walk on a battlefield. Maybe y'all don't realize it, but everywhere y'all go, y'all make a battlefield. So thanks ain't necessary, soldier. But what is necessary is that you tell me why you playing against Bigg. That's the nigga I'm really fuckin' with, all right. Let's not get it twisted," she said straight out, not trying to sound cool, but so he understood her role and where she stood.

Rob felt that, for all she'd done, she deserved to know, so she could make her decision. "Look, at this point, I got to go on what those killers said. They called Reignah a snitch and said Butch name. That's Fox partner. I think I know who sent them, and I don't know who's involved, so I'm taking precaution."

"That's Bigg, Rob," she said, looking over at him.

"That's my life they almost took back there. Those assassins were trained. They had me dazed, down, and secured in seconds and went straight to work. You were not what they expected. They killed Reignah. Shot her in the head, and didn't blink," he said in pain. Then he was silent. Nothing for about two minutes.

"That's what I saw. I heard the crash in the bathroom and her first scream. I got the gun and ran downstairs and eased in the back door. I slid around the corner, and *Boom!* he did it. I fired off the shots. I keep seeing the same picture. I finally started being able to sleep from all the shit we been going through with this war, and all the cruel, inhumane things that went on, and now I got a new picture flash.

"And, you right, they were trained. They had silencers for a .44 special. They call them the Bulldog. You can't even get them right now and their silencers. Oh my God!" she said, showing her love of weaponry. "So what's the plan? We going to Virginia to see Bigg?"

"No, we going to D.C. Then we gonna call Bigg." Rob leaned back and rested. He needed something. IIe felt like his mind was getting ready to explode. He ended up dozing off.

Hours later, Carol Anne was pulling into a hotel outside of North Lake Mall in Macon, GA. It was almost noon. She'd driven all night and couldn't anymore. She went in and got a room. She went in the bathroom and showered. She felt refreshed, but still tired, and lay across the bed in the same clothes she had on.

Rob cleaned his wounds that still hadn't been ad-

dressed. He took a long, hot shower, thoughts of revenge still eating at him. He couldn't believe Reignah
was gone. He felt lost. He had to get to D.C.

After he showered, he felt refreshed and told Carol
Anne that he'd drive, she could sleep in the car.

Chapter Twenty-two

It had been a long week, and now there I was faced with this shit—Rob fucking up the connect, with no idea if Fox was gonna even deal with us again. I told him not to try and play them Haitians against each other. Now I was possibly fucked. I had two days to find out my fate and where I stood. Then I'd have to wait for Fox to go get product and get it to me. And we knew Fox's prices weren't like Wyi-Z's.

I looked over at Ree-Ree's obituary sitting right in the middle of the coffee table. The picture her mom used was my favorite. She looked beautiful on the front, just as she did in the casket that gloomy past Monday.

The wake was hard on everybody Sunday night, but the funeral was a sight to see. I wasn't prepared for what came about, her moms, sisters, cousins, all falling out screaming. I had let LB sit with his grandmother, because she'd had him since the death of his mom. I thought he'd found security over there.

When all the commotion started, he was standing there crying hard, not because of his mother's death, but because he was lost. He didn't know what was going on and was scared.

I sat with the family up front, next to NaVante and Shamar. I was a ways from him when he caught my eye through the havoc. I moved quickly as if he was lost in a mall. I grabbed him and scooped him up.

He opened his teary eyes and saw that it was me and yelled, "Daddy, I was scared. Please don't leave me no more. Please." And he threw his arms around my neck and squeezed as if he was holding on for dear life.

"All right, son, I got you. You okay," I said, reassuring him. I sat back down with him.

"Mommy gone?"

"Yes, she's gone to be with God. See, God needs angels, and He only picks the best people to turn into angels. So you know your mommy was the best, right."

"Right," he answered.

"We gonna be all right. Promise you," I told him. The tears filled my eyes, and I squeezed him.

After the funeral, everyone went back to my house, where everything was laid out. All he wanted was to go to his room and chill.

When everyone began leaving, he hid in the closet, hoping they would forget him. We laughed, but I felt him and told him that he was all right. "I got him," I said, but I didn't know for how long. I just didn't know.

The following day, me and NaVante went to bring Basan home. LB stayed at the house with Shamar. The doctors gave us all the medicines to give Basan and the ointment to put on his little body, which was healing. After I signed mad papers, they said one of us was gonna have to sit in the wheelchair and be rolled out with the baby. Hospital rules.

NaVante looked at me and smiled.

"I'm not gonna be rolled out of here," I said.

"No problem. I will," she said, sitting in the wheelchair.

They placed Basan in her arms, and she cradled him close in her arms, just like a mother. Amazingly, he opened his eyes, looked at me, then stared at her and didn't take his eyes off her til we got down and put him in the car seat. We went home, and she jumped out the car to go open the door.

"Better come get this little nigga, so I can get this shit out the car. He staring at you like he don't know who the hell I am." I laughed as I handed her Basan.

"Give him here. I got him," she said, staring down at him. "I got you. Yes, auntie do," she said in baby talk.

The first couple days he stayed in his crib in his room, and every time he made a sound, we both rushed to his bedside. Most of the feedings, she did. The changing, she did, dressing and bathing him, she did, and between naps, she just sat and stared at him in amazement. Then she would talk and talk as if he could understand.

Couple times, I caught her talking Spanish to him, and I let her know that we only spoke English around here, even though I wanted him to learn Spanish too. She would just smile and keep on going.

After a few days, I realized she started feeding him and bathing him, then taking him in her room and laying him beside her.

By Friday, she had a system going, not only for Basan, but for LB too.

I remember the first night LB came home. Ree-Ree would let him stay up until he fell asleep. She would run the streets, always late coming home from her moms, girlfriend's, or somewhere, but NaVante always told her she was wrong, that he needed a to go to bed at a particular time.

So when we were looking at TV that Monday night after everyone had left, it was about 8:10 when she said, "Somebody need to get a bath and get ready for bed."

LB looked around as if she was just talking.

"Hey, bath time now," she said directly to him, and he went to remove his clothes.

She got up to run his water in his room.

By 8:30 he was in his bed, allowed to look at TV for thirty minutes before it went off.

I was impressed by her actions. She stood in and helped out a lot. In fact, I slowly began to see her trying to run my house.

Now here she was on this Friday night sitting beside me as we looked at one of Tyler Perry's new movies.

"I love Madea," she said as she walked back in the living room with popcorn.

"All these nigga's movies on point, and he getting paid, from the stage to the screen." I dumped the tobacco from the Backwoods and loaded it up with Kush. I put it to my lips and reached for my lighter.

NaVante grabbed it off the table and stood up. "Outside," she said softly.

I gave her a look that said, "Stop playing."

"*No más en la casa.*"

"What? I got no more in what?"

"Not in the house," she said, standing by the back patio door.

I got up and walked out. We stood on the large wooden deck I had built. I reached for the lighter, and she reached for the "Back." I gave it to her.

She lit it, took three deep pulls, and passed it.

"Needed that, huh?"

"Helps me relax, sleep a little better." She smiled. She pulled the door open to hear something. "Was that my phone?"

I went inside to get it off the counter and brought it to her.

She looked at it and ignored it. Another call came through. She turned it on silent.

"That's not right," I said.

"What ain't right?"

"To ignore him. To sit here in front of me and shit on your man."

She looked at me funny.

"Yeah! To ignore his call in front of me, says what?" I asked. "If I liked you like that, it would tell me you don't respect the nigga that's calling, and the door is open for me to try and fuck. I'm not gonna sugarcoat shit while I'm talking to you . . . because some things you shouldn't do."

"Well, some things he shouldn't do. All he gonna do is fuss, put me down, and try to make me feel like shit."

"Really? And how is that?"

"Because he think I'm fuckin' you. He think something going on. He feel I should not be here with you alone, that some shit got to be popping!"

"So for that you ignore him, instead of answering and letting him know what it is?" I frowned.

"He don't hear me, and he keep making accusations."

"You fine as hell. You staying with a nigga that's fine as hell, with all the things in life that could make your life very comfortable. Now, even though I'm your cousin's man, he know, to most men, that means nothing. He know other men desire you, and he's paranoid and jealous that you might be sad or hurt enough to fall into my arms. Too many things can happen behind closed doors. And when you don't know, it's mind-wrenching."

"Yeah, but I been with him a long time, and he should know me. I ain't like that."

"Like what? You ain't a woman? You don't get lonesome? You don't get hurt and sad, and would love to have someone's arms wrapped around you? And we know anybody can't get ya, but there's that nigga, that nigga that's too fuckin' cool."

We both smiled.

"No matter how I feel, that's not gonna make me sleep with you. I got to care, and I got to be single."

"I heard that. Seem like you on your way, doing that shit. Is that what you want?"

"No, but I'm tired of being shitted on. That, I'm not gonna go for, especially when nothing going on. I can't help his insecurities."

"Well, if my girl was living with a nigga, I would have the same problem."

"You wouldn't believe her?" She stared at me for an answer.

"I would try, but it will be real hard. And this is the shit. Even after you move out, I still don't know if I'll ever trust you, because I'll never know what truly happened. I won't know the secrets y'all have. I will feel he's seen you in the way that I have."

"What? You crazy, Bigg." She pulled on the Backwoods.

"No, I'm not. You just don't know how men think. Women think it's all about giving up the pussy, but it's about everything else. You are giving me everything, but that. Okay, he pictured me being with you, and it drove him crazy, but he also thinks about me and you sitting around, looking at Madea on the couch. That's what you do with your man. He tries to picture what you got on around me, what you put on after you come out the shower, what you look like before going to bed, what you look like in the morning. What underclothes you wearing. What you're going through. How your day was. All of this you supposed to share with your man, not with me. He feels no other man but him should know any of these things about you. That's all his perks of being your man. And here you are, living with me. I say all this not for you to run back to him, but for you to see how he's looking at it. Do whatever to help him feel secure," I said seriously.

Yes, I was starting to feel her, but if she came my way, she was a keeper and that's how I would treat her, so I needed her to be free and single, no obstacles.

"That's what you feel? If I explain it, he'll understand?"

"Yeah! If you don't want to lose him. You been with him a minute, right?"

"Yeah."

"And he'll do anything for you and give you anything, right?"

"He'll try, but he can't give me everything."

"In time he will," I said to her. "He gonna make it. Give him time."

"Nothing can change this. I can't have kids, so he

can't give me that. Can he, Bigg? Can he?" NaVante walked back inside.

I finished the *L* and followed her. She was sitting on the couch eating popcorn with tears in her eyes. I sat down beside her and hugged her, and she relaxed in my arms as we finished looking at Madea.

The following morning I woke to breakfast flowing with NaVante doing her thing in the kitchen. She was on the phone as I made my way to the kitchen and poured some juice. My mind was on Rob and our connect.

I grabbed my phone and walked to the patio and called our connect. I needed to know what went wrong.

"What up, Bigg? Long time," Wyi-Z said.

"You know, I let my man handle the business in Miami."

"Yeah, yeah! Well, your man gone, right. I hope him gone, because I hear him on the news. They kill his girl, but he kill two assassins."

"Yeah! Assassins. He said the Haitian posse destroyed his life and wife."

"No, no, not the Posse work," Wyi-Z said. "Definitely not the Posse work."

"I need to see you then."

"What ya need? I know you love the new price, Bigg."

"That's why I'm coming. Coming to get my ID and bring good money. You know I double count." I wondered about the new price, but I didn't want him to know Rob was getting me.

"Yeah, yeah! Double count. Make sure a hundred and thirty grand in the bag," Wyi-Z said.

"Don't I know. How long it's been now?"

"You right. After three months you should know," he said.

My mind began to race. This cat dropped the price by $3,500 per kilo, and Rob never said shit. So he was pocketing $35,000 every two weeks. My boy was making $70,000 a month off me. And he lied about the Haitians. *What the fuck Rob got going on?*

I called his phone. No answer. Called Carol Anne. No answer.

My appetite was out the window. I couldn't believe this. *Not my nigga.* I pulled him in and showed him. I got Carol Anne so he could roll tight. I didn't believe this nigga did this to me, lied to my face.

Seventy grand a month for three to four months. Oh, hell naw! He was paying for this $210,000. He must've lost his mind, because he was sure gonna lose his life. If it wasn't the Haitians work, then who did he piss off for them to come and kill Reignah? This was too serious. And how did they miss him?

I'd find out in the next couple days what all this was about, but I was gonna give him one last opportunity to come clean with me before doing what his other enemies couldn't. My man had me fucked up.

I walked back inside to food on the table. This, I was all right with—bacon, fried eggs, cheese on toast, and a big-ass glass of Tropicana with mango.

LB sat on the floor, looking at cartoons on the 52-inch flat-screen Sony, and NaVante sat holding Basan, talking to my sons in Spanish, making hand gestures, making him smile.

I walked over and touched her shoulder, and she reached up and touched my hand.

I said a silent prayer, "God touch her, for she is doing a lot. Touch my sons and watch over them. And for all

I do, all I can say is guide me. Wrap me in Your arms and let no harm come to me or my family. Amen!"

"Did you pack up all Ree-Ree things?" I asked Na-Vante.

"Yes, in suitcases, and the shoes are in the bag," she said softly.

"Thank you. Her cousin Barbeda should come by soon."

"I know Barbeda. She was at the funeral," she said, going to lay Basan down. "I'm going to get myself together, be back down in a bit," she said and disappeared upstairs.

Chapter Twenty-three

Rob had reached Arlington and stopped to get a room Saturday night. He rode out to see where Fox rested, and if he had left out for Virginia Beach. Rob noticed he was still home as he passed the beautiful custom-built home in the exclusive neighborhood in Alexandria. He left with plans in his head that would come together tomorrow. He headed back to the hotel to get Carol Anne, so they could get something to eat and relax. Tomorrow would be a big day.

Fox relaxed, holding his wife. It was 2:00 a.m., and he was just dozing off. He had made love to Joy about an hour ago, and she fell asleep in his arms and hadn't moved. He had concerns about his meeting with Bigg and Rob. He didn't know if Rob truly felt the Haitians tried to kill him, or if he knew it was him. Did Bigg know what was going on? Did he see through it all and was on Rob's side, feeling his life was next on the line? This entire thing had him sick, but he made his choice to get to Bigg early and come clean. He drifted off to sleep holding his wife like she might get away.

Joy lay turned away, snuggled under her husband, her eyes shut, but she was wide-awake. She could feel his uneasiness, but she knew now wasn't the time. He had to handle his business and straighten things out.

Fox nodded off, but he never went into a deep sleep. He opened his eyes at the sounds of Joy getting ready for church. He sat up, and the beautiful sight of his wife sent chills through his body.

"I love you, baby. I truly love you," he said, staring at her in the beige Ann Taylor skirt suit and Nine West black heels. He continued to stare taking her in, all of her.

"Love you too, baby." Joy walked over and gave him a kiss. "You'll be gone when I get out of church?"

"Yeah! Get on down here and handle this shit, and I'm back tonight, I hope."

"Better be. Call me," she said, walking over and putting on her accessories.

"You be careful, Joy," he said seriously. "Be careful out there."

"I always am," she said, leaving out the room. "Later, sweetie." She headed down the stairs.

Fox got up to get himself together. After a shower and a bite to eat, he looked around at his home and got a funny feeling, but he pushed it to the side, due to all the shit going on in his life. He jumped in his 300M and hit the road, headed to Virginia Beach.

Rob sat in the dark green Buick LeSabre down and across the street, getting a full view of Fox's home. He'd been out there since 7:00 a.m. He hadn't been able to sleep at all. He was feeling as if his whole life had hit a brick wall. He hurt inside. He felt like he was gonna have a breakdown, all in the name of love and revenge.

His eyes widened when he saw the garage door open and the Escalade truck pull out. He could see it was Joy driving, and in the back seat sat Fox's precious daughter that he loved with his every breath and latched onto for dear life after the loss of his son.

Rob watched her back out as the garage door went down, and she disappeared down the street. He sat patiently as his stomach turned and his heart hurt.

Rob couldn't believe Reignah was gone. The last several months had been a blast. He'd forgotten all about being a fugitive. She brought joy and purpose. Now he had nothing again, all because of his man.

A couple hours passed, and he finally saw the garage open again, and out came the 300M. *Same one he had at Bink funeral*, Rob thought. He watched as the garage door shut and the Chrysler 300 made its way around the corner and vanished.

He looked at his watch, as time crept by. An hour passed, and he put his on black gloves.

Another hour passed, while he took his time exploring the area and the activity going on.

Around two o'clock, he moved and parked the stolen Buick in front of the garage door on the right side where the Chrysler was parked. As he exited the car, he realized that all the butterflies, all the hurt, and all the anger wasn't there. It was no longer a part of him at this time. He was finally focused on his mission and in total control.

Me and Navante were standing on the deck sharing the haze-filled Backwoods and a drink while Basan slept. LB had gone back to his grandmother last night. She had something planned for their family.

Navante was saying how hard it was gonna be to leave. I agreed because she'd been such a great help taking care of my boy, just like his mother would have, and that was a blessing to me.

As our conversation began to get deeper, a knock came at the door, and then a shake, checking to see if it was unlocked to let himself in, but safety was first in my world now.

We walked inside to see who it was, and were both surprised at Fox's early arrival.

"Hello."

Navante opened the door after looking at me, wondering who this was, but she had an idea from us talking. She had become my friend, and we were having a lot of in-depth conversations.

"Hello. How are you?" Fox looked at her, wondering who she was.

"What up, partner?" I said, giving him a pound and a hug.

Fox watched NaVante walk away in the Juicy Couture sweat pants and T-shirt. "Damn, who's that?" he asked.

"Navy. Ree-Ree sister. Ree-Ree died giving birth to my son about three weeks ago. So I been going through the storm."

The jokes and smirks went out the window, and the serious captain we knew appeared. "Sorry, Bigg. I'm really sorry to hear that," he said sadly.

I knew he understood the death of a close one. "I'm dealing with it," I said. "Why you here so early? I wasn't expecting you til eight. I know you ain't come here to hang out."

"Naw, I got to tell you some serious shit. It's a long fucked-up story."

"Let me get two beers, and you give me the fast, short version. I don't need to hear a lot of shit."

I was getting ready to walk inside when NaVante came to the door. "Bigg, would you and your company like anything?" she asked pleasantly.

"Two of those Red Stripes," I said smiling.

Fox just stared at her and smiled then looked at me. "What is she? Puerto Rican, Mexican, something Spanish?" he asked, smirking.

"Dominican. They all speak that shit we don't understand."

"She speak Spanish?"

"Hell, yeah!" I said, looking at him. "She be sitting around talking to my son in Spanish, on the phone with her peoples, her man."

"Damn! I know he killing that shit," he said.

Fox got quiet as she came back out and handed us the beers. "Thank you," he said, staring at her. "I'm Fox. And you are?" He smiled.

"NaVante, and it's nice meeting you." She smiled then slowly turned and walked back inside.

I smiled at Fox when he looked at me.

He shook his head. "My wife beautiful, but NaVante, if she come out here and say, 'Leave your wife, I got you, *papi*,' if she say that, I'm moving in. I won't leave, and I'll pay the mortgage on the first." He laughed.

With sweats, hair pulled back, and no makeup, she was gorgeous, and to me she was down-to-earth. I really didn't care for the flirtatious remarks toward her. I felt she was on a different level. I wanted to say, "Respect her like you would my baby's mother," but I knew I would be out of line from every angle, but I couldn't help how I felt.

"The people I go to said Rob girl was a snitch and they had to be dealt with, or they were gonna kill all of us and our families," Fox said.

"They gonna kill who?" I asked, standing straight up.

"They know everybody I been dealing with," Fox explained. "And they said they would kill everybody if I didn't kill Rob and Reignah."

I thought Fox had put my family in danger by not telling me earlier. "Why you ain't come to us and say nothing? They may try and kill everybody anyway. What's gonna stop them?"

"We started together, man, me, Bink, Rob, and Sid. You showed us this shit, coming out of Fort Bragg. This shit wasn't on base. I think you made a bad decision that you got to live with, because you killed his girl, and she was pregnant. Whoever you sent was gonna kill him, but someone intervened, and he made an escape. Right now, he think it was the Haitians that did it. I don't know what to tell you, Fox. Just be careful. But I can say, my house ain't for y'all to be meeting. We got to carry this somewhere else. If something ain't right, it won't happen around here, because you don't know what he know and what they said before they killed his girl."

"Yeah! It's been eating at me, but I had no choice. I had to make a decision."

"Right now, I'm worried about my family," I said. "If your peoples know what they know, they are well connected. That's why I like doing my own thing. It's all on me."

I felt like I was now on my own, with my connect. But why did Rob want to meet at my house? *He must think I had something to do with this shit.* I'd see, but I was getting out of here.

Fox stood in a deep stare. He didn't know that if he came to me a week ago, he would've gotten a different reaction, but since my partner Rob wanted to rob me, of all my people, today I could care less if he was living or not.

"My worry is my family. I should've killed y'all niggas a long time ago, like Ree-Ree said. Yo, call Rob, and y'all get together on things. I've got some shit to do and secure in my family. It's nothing to say or do right now, until things are clear," I said standing up straight, staring in his eyes.

He stood up straight, almost at attention, and finished his beer. "I'ma get outta here. I'll call him and see where I can meet him, and play it by ear."

"Be easy, sir," I said, not feeling shit for this man anymore.

I knew why I felt that Rob deserved to be executed, but Reignah wasn't no snitch, and that was bad judgment on Fox's part.

Fox left out and got in his car and pulled off. He called back moments later, letting me know Rob didn't answer his phone and that if he contacted me, to tell him he was getting a room at the downtown Marriott. I guess he wanted to deal with Rob face to face, man to man, soldier to soldier.

I called my mom and told her to call Sidney's mom and let her know I needed to holler at him. He'd been back from Afghanistan for six weeks, and I hadn't heard from or seen him.

It wasn't long before he called me back.

We talked briefly, and I let him know all that was going on with the streets and life. He was bothered by the gentlemen Fox worked for, and that they'd make such a threat. We said our good-byes, knowing I would see him soon.

Chapter Twenty-four

Rob eased into the garage before the door came down. He lay low on the passenger side, while Joy took her time getting out the truck.

Joy was full of the spirit, singing and rejoicing, appreciating all that she'd gotten from the morning service. She walked around the passenger side to let her daughter out of the car seat and jumped at the sight of Rob. Her eyes widened as she jetted toward the door, forgetting about her child. She tried to run, but Rob caught her and tripped her.

Before she could get up, he ran over to her and threw his left arm around her neck, and his knee in her back. In seconds he had choked her out, and she lay, not moving. He grabbed the back of her suit jacket and dragged her into the house.

Then he went back outside and got her daughter, brought her in the house, and told her to go to her room. She cried but did as she was told.

Joy was coming to, so Rob tied her hands and feet

then gagged her with a washcloth and duct tape. He watched her wriggle on the floor like a fish out of water. She watched him with terrified eyes, just as Reignah did, the exact same.

Joy's daughter came back downstairs and began screaming at the sight of her mom laying on the floor, bound and gagged. She let out a deafening scream, which stopped instantly when Rob kicked her in her back, sending her 60 lbs. flying across the room into her mother. She lay gasping for air.

Rob waited patiently, with mother and daughter tied up in the floor.

As the sun went down and dusk settled in, Rob opened the garage door and pulled in the stolen car. He then pulled Joy into the garage and threw her in the trunk, then got the child and threw her on top of her. He shut the trunk, opened the garage door, and took off, headed to my house.

When he reached Hampton, he made a call.

Rob called me, and I told him that Fox was downtown at the Marriott.

Then he said to me with a dry, raspy voice, "Yo, Bigg, did you know about that nigga trying to kill me and being responsible for Reignah?"

"Naw, Rob. That's new shit," I said. "Are you sure? Thought you said it was the Haitians?"

"After seeing my girl die, I didn't know who to trust. But this dude is gonna pay. When I call you, Bigg, answer your phone. I'll be in Norfolk in about thirty minutes."

Rob finally answered Joy's phone when he saw Fox's number. Fox had called fifty times, but Rob never answered.

"What up, dog?" Rob answered.

"I got the wrong number," Fox said. "My bad."

"No, you don't. I'm Joy new man. She ain't talking no more. She tied up."

"What's going on? Who the fuck is this?"

"Who the fuck is this? This is Rob, baby. What's going on? I'm coming to talk to you. I will be in front of the Marriott in ten minutes."

"Where the fuck is my wife? And how you get her phone?" Fox said, gritting his teeth. He was now mad as hell that he didn't go handle this shit himself. Butch had fucked up.

"Calm down. I know where my future wife and child at. Do you know, Fox?"

Fox said nothing.

"Don't worry, yours not with mine yet. I need to see you first. Be sitting in the front, in your car, and follow me," Rob said calmly.

"Nothing better not—"

"What you say? Say another word, and it will be a shame what this nigga do to your bitch!" Rob yelled. *Simple muthafucka trying to call shots.*

Rob pulled in front of the Marriott and saw Fox. He blew once, and Fox pulled behind him and called me. He told me he was going over by the bus station in Norfolk.

I was close by downtown, so I went by the bus station, just in time to see Fox following Rob. "What the fuck is he doing?" I asked.

"He finding a good spot," Sidney said. "He going up by the city zoo."

"How you know? Shut the hell up!" I said, fucking with Sid.

I followed them, and they turned right by the city zoo. I looked at Sidney. "How did you get to me so fast? And how you know what's going on?"

"Rob called me, asked me a few things, and I told him how to go about it. I don't like Fox, and never have. That's your man. Look at the shit he done caused. He would've killed you too if those crackers he fuck with told him to," Sidney said.

"I know now. Shit!"

I watched Rob come to a stop in the darkness, with only street lights to guide him through. I stopped behind Fox and got out the car. I saw Fox exit the car quickly, while Rob slowly got out the car and walked to the side.

I stepped up beside them, almost looking like a referee.

"One question, dog. Why?" Rob asked.

"It came from up high. It wasn't my decision. Your girl was gonna set you up, and I couldn't let all of us fall for your love of pussy," Fox said. "She wasn't your wife. Find another one."

"She was gonna be, and she had my child in her. And, just to let you know, we were serving her cousin that's on the run. Little nigga still doing his thing on the run in Hampton. That's where I ran into Sid." Rob looked at me.

I just stood there looking at both my longtime friends.

"Rob, I'm sorry," Fox said, "but we couldn't take the chance. Now she's gone, problem over with. Now let's get money. Don't let girls come between what we had."

"All right. I just want you to hear those words after you've seen what I've seen." Rob threw Fox the keys and stepped back. "Open the trunk," he said.

My stomach began to churn. I didn't know what to expect as Fox popped the trunk. His wife, drenched from the hot trunk, lay motionless, bound and gagged, not moving with her eyes open, and his daughter was slumped across her, throat cut from ear to ear.

Fox fell to his knees. "Uh! Uh! Uh! Uh! Uh!"

Rob didn't expect her to die, but she had suffocated on the three-hour trip. He wanted to kill her in front of Fox, so he could feel his pain. But he realized the pain Fox was feeling had already killed him.

I stepped back just in time to see Fox jump to his feet at Rob, but Rob was prepared. It happened so quick.

Fox lunged at Rob, and as his hands hit Rob's neck, he felt the heat in his stomach then his chest, and his eyes fell shut as his body fell over onto his wife and child.

My eyes widened at the scene unraveling in front of me. I was there because I was gonna confront Rob, but I was shaken by the scene.

Rob stood with the same .45 with the silencer that they used to kill his girl. He pushed the rest of Fox's body in the trunk with his family and shut it. He looked at me. "Problem solved," he said.

"One of them. What about my two hundred and ten thousand?" I said, finally forcing it out.

"What?" Rob said.

"I talked to Wyi-Z. You been getting me, Rob. Why?"

"It's like this, Bigg—"

Sidney hit him up with two shots to his head, and we both watched his body fall.

My whole life flashed before my eyes, but I never blinked.

"Let's go," Sidney said as he climbed in my car.

I never hesitated as I jumped in the driver's seat and made my way down Granby Street, headed home. "So how long you been here?" I asked.

"In Hampton, a month. In the States too," he said.

I asked seriously, "You told him to do what he did, Sidney?"

"I told him go in his house and hold them. Call Fox and make him come home then kill him. I never said shit about putting that man family in a trunk and driving across the state. Come on, Bigg," he said, like it was unbelievable

"Like you won't do that shit. Nigga, you kill with no remorse, no thought. That's dangerous. You need prayer," I said.

"I'm what the military made."

My phone rang just then. The number was unfamiliar. I answered, "Hello," wondering who it could be.

"Hey, Bigg. It's Carol Anne," she said, as if she was unsure of me.

I had also called her phone. "You weren't answering. Where are you?"

"I'm in D.C. waiting on Rob. He left me at the hotel, but he been gone all day."

"Why you at a hotel?" I asked.

"People came to get him. They killed Reignah, and I saved him. We left and came to D.C. He left early, and I been here. What's up?" she asked, looking for guidance.

I looked at Sidney. He knew and heard all that was going on.

"Tell her to come to Virginia Beach," Sidney said, shaking his head to a new joint by Jadakiss. "We gonna be here a minute."

"Come to Virginia Beach, get a room on the strip,

and just chill out, enjoy yourself. You got money?" I asked.

"I got a car, money, drugs, guns, too much shit to be moving around. This Rob stuff."

"Bring everything to me. When you pass the Norfolk Airport exit, look for North Hampton Boulevard exit, and get a room at Lake Wright Hotel. Then call me."

"See you soon," she said and hung up.

"Now what exactly is she gonna do here?" I asked out loud.

"She gonna work. We gonna put her with Erica, Fox girl," Sidney said.

"What about Butch?"

"No, we only deal with Erica. She deal with Butch. And we gonna be coming with Carol Anne. People gonna think you don't exist," Sidney said. "Let me tell you something, Bigg. I stood back and let all this play out. I just prayed you wouldn't get killed in the process. You got your bumps, bruises, and your scars, but you were running with reckless men.

"Fox was a leader, but not for these streets. Bink allowed his woman to take over his life. He wanted to catch her fucking around so bad, he used to say it to me. And look what happened when he did.

"Rob was a soldier," he said, looking at me. "Your boy Rob was a true soldier. And I can say I was wrong, because I thought he would be here with you."

"Yeah!" I said softly, catching a lump in my throat and a knot in my stomach, taking away any desire for eating.

I took a deep breath as if my heart had skipped a beat for my close, dear friend that made him take his life for change. We were better than that.

Sidney looked at me. "But if he robbed you, and you

lost trust in him because of his direct actions to you, I'm with you. And you made a decision."

"*You* made the decision for me," I said.

"Did you think Rob would've killed you when you said something about the money?" he asked.

"Naw, I don't think so. But I was gonna lay him down."

"I'm gonna say this, and we done with it, Bigg. I did him because you a soldier, and Rob a soldier, but I don't know, leave it at that, I just don't know," he said, shaking his head and smiling.

I smiled because, for real, I didn't know either.

My mind drifted to NaVante. I'd told her mostly what was going on, not really wanting to involve her in my business. But I knew, when I left with Sidney, anything could've happened, so I made her promise that she would look after Basan and raise him as if he was hers. She'd stood in front of me with tears in her eyes and promised. I even told her where my money was, every cent I'd made and had to my name for her and my boy. I had to put my trust in someone. I never thought it would be Ree-Ree's sister.

As we rode in silence, I thought about all that had taken place. I realized the life I had chosen was so unpredictable. It was crazy, but with my connect in Miami, and Sidney by my side, I was going to the top.

I pulled up at the house and walked inside. NaVante was standing there holding Basan. She laid him down and came over to me and gave me a hug like I couldn't believe. She squeezed me and allowed her body to fold and press into mine as if I was holding her up.

It wasn't the first time I hugged her, but it was the first time I truly felt her. She didn't seem to want to let go, and I didn't either. It was a moment, a memorable moment.

We slowly broke our tight embrace.

NaVante stared into my eyes and smiled. *"Prométame usted no me espantarás como eso otra vez*, Bigg. *Te necesitamos."*

"Prométame usted no nos dejarás, NaVante. Te necesitamos."